BROKEN SINGLE DADDY'S BABY

CALLIE STEVENS

1

DEREK

I groan in the front seat of the car as my four-year-old son kicks my seat repeatedly.

"Eli, I swear to God, I will turn this car around."

"No!" six-year-old Maggie yelps. "I want a cake pop, Daddy!"

"Cake, cake, cake," Eli chants.

These two are more than just a handful and all I want is to go and grab some coffee before work. Unfortunately, the daycare doesn't open until seven and I'm already wary about leaving them there just as drop-ins. Maggie and Eli are great kids, but they can be a little rambunctious.

Eli kicks my seat again and I take in a deep breath and count to ten. I'm what many people would call a "permissive" parent, and I practice gentle parenting as much as I can, but right now, I feel like my head might explode.

"Cake pops," I mutter, and Eli finally stops kicking my seat and favors me with a smile, showing his little teeth.

"Cake pops and a strawberry milkshake!" Maggie cries, as if she'll *die* if she doesn't get those two things immediately.

"Only if you two are good," I say firmly, and Eli pouts.

"Eli in trouble, Daddy?" he asks me, holding out his arms for me to pick him up after I get out of the car and open the back door.

My heart seems to swell two sizes at the look of him, his green eyes so much like mine.

"Not in trouble, Eli. Just be good in the shop, okay?"

"Okay," he says easily, wrapping his legs around my hip as I lift him out of his car seat.

Maggie is already trying to unbuckle herself from the safety seat, so I hurry over to help, but she wants none of that.

"I can do it, Daddy. I'm a big girl," she says, and her little tongue is peeking out at all the effort she is making. She is starting to get frustrated and that is not good. For any of us.

"You know?" I tell her. "Even I struggle with that sometimes, so maybe we can do it together and you can help me?"

She looks at me suspiciously at first, but then smiles and says, "Okay, Daddy. I can help you."

I sigh inwardly in relief that the crisis was averted and let her hands settle on mine as I finally unbuckle her, pretending to expend a lot of effort along the process, causing her to giggle the whole time.

Once we are done, she insists on getting off the chair by herself and I take her hand in mine as soon as she is out of the car.

She looks up at me with her chin upturned. "I can walk by *myself*," she says firmly, but I keep hold of her hand.

"I know, honey. But I'm getting old and I can't do it by myself, or while I'm carrying Eli here, so please keep holding my hand and help me, okay?"

She is getting more independent by the hour, almost,

but I know she'll do anything for me and Eli, so I have to play all the cards I can to make the whole process easier and still keep her safe, because there is no way a six-year-old should be crossing a road by herself, if there is an adult close by. Especially not my baby girl when I'm right here to keep her safe.

So, holding her hand, I walk right beside her as she looks both ways dutifully and walks across the pedestrian crosswalk.

Taking a four-year-old and a six-year-old to the coffee shop at six in the morning isn't exactly my idea of a great time, but I'm sort of between childcares. My parents kept the kids for me for a long time after Suzanna left, but they're getting older and it's hard for them to chase them around.

So, for today, I'm trying a drop-in daycare to see how the kids do. I'll need a long-term solution, and fast, but it takes time to decide who you want to watch your children.

They've been through so much already.

Eli scrambles to get down and he runs immediately to the cake display, pointing at a big piece of cheesecake. "Cake!" he shouts and starts banging his little fist on the glass like waiting for someone to open it or ask who it is from the other side.

"Eli, please stop banging the glass. You'll break it. Also, cheesecake for breakfast, buddy? I don't think so," I grumble under my breath, taking his hand and pulling him away from the display case.

"We have to wait in line, Eli," Maggie says matter-of-factly, and Eli, who looks up to his sister, obediently goes to take her hand and wait in line ahead of me, but the lure of the display counter seems too big of a temptation and in seconds, both of them are running and gluing their faces to the glass, each pointing at different treats, apparently trying to beat each other at who finds the best one.

A young woman is in line ahead of me, wearing a pair of jeans and a crop-top. She has a dirty blonde high ponytail. She is pushed back, almost bumping into me, when Maggie and Eli crowd in front of her, as she's waiting for her order.

I hold her up and away from me, and when she looks back to both apologize and thank me, I realize she is much younger than I expected. The kids are all up in her space now, talking a mile a minute and she has to walk around them to get to the counter now.

Horrified, I call "Maggie, Eli, please come back here. We have to wait our turn in line or no cake pops for you." The kids look at me as if I'm an ogre depriving them of their most treasured possession. Then to the woman I say, "Sorry. My kids don't know what personal space is."

"It's all right," she says, smiling down at them.

Eli looks dejected, and having been scolded, Maggie is now mad. She gives the woman a death glare that I swear only six-year-olds are capable of.

"What's your name?" the woman asks her undeterred by her attitude, and Maggie looks down before answering.

"Margaret," she mumbles. "Margaret Veronica Ledderman."

"What a big girl name!" the woman says brightly.

Maggie looks at her and her eyes are shining. "I like when people call me Maggie," she says shyly, and I blink down at her, surprised. Maggie doesn't like speaking to people, and she's usually either pretty standoffish or pretty shy depending on the person.

The woman crouches down to Maggie's level and offers her hand. When Maggie takes it, she shakes her hand firmly. "I'm Kenna," she says.

Eli just stares at her with wide green eyes. "Eli," he says, simple enough, and I bite my lip to keep from laughing.

"We should probably leave this lovely young woman alone," I say, taking their hands. "Why don't you two find us a table?"

"Cake?" Eli asks hopefully.

"Cake *pops*," I say, unwilling to let him have cheesecake this early in the morning even if he did eat eggs and drink some orange juice before we left the house.

Eli doesn't complain and Maggie drags him toward a seat near the window.

I turn back to the young woman, smiling. "I really am sorry about that," I say, and she waves a hand dismissively.

"It was no problem at all. They're adorable," she says with a bright smile.

She's quite pretty, although *way* too young for me. She has bright blue eyes and a pretty, crooked smile.

"Kenna, was it?" I ask, just to be polite. I feel awkward in these kinds of social situations. In high school, Suzanna pursued me like a Pitbull, and I'd gotten into a relationship with her that had spanned nearly thirteen years. I'm okay fraternizing at work, but it's never more than friendly banter or innocent flirting with women I know are unavailable. And they know I'm unavailable too and it's all for fun. Outside of work, though, I get all awkward and tongue-tied.

"That's me," she says, sounding bubbly.

"I'm Derek," I say. "Since my kids didn't introduce me." It sounds dumb even to my own ears, but Kenna smiles.

"Nice to meet you," she says quietly, and then grabs her order from the barista when they call her name.

I stare at her for a moment longer before looking toward the barista, almost glad when Kenna walks away that I don't have to keep up conversation, because I kind of suck at it.

The kids are bouncing around near the window, making a ruckus and just being kids, honestly, but a few people there are starting to give them the looks. So, I order quickly and head over toward them.

I pull out a couple of sheets of paper from my briefcase and some crayons that I keep in there for the kids and Eli and Maggie both begin to draw. Eli nearly draws on the tabletop, too, but thank God they're erasable crayons.

Eli pauses after a few moments, looking around, and I freeze, thinking he's probably going to go wild waiting for his cake pop. Turns out I'm looking at the wrong kid, because Maggie turns over the sugar container and it spills all over the table as they finally call my name for the cake pops, strawberry smoothies, and latte.

"Shit," I mutter.

"Daddy, you said a bad word." *Shit!* I almost said it again.

"Sorry, honey. Daddy—" At that second, Eli starts to fuss too.

"Yellow!" he screams, pointing at his sister.

She shakes her head, holding the crayon to her chest and says, "U-hu. I need it, pick another color."

"YELLOW!" he screams louder.

"No!" she screams back, and I'm really considering just grabbing them both and leaving this place without the cake pops, just cutting my loses.

"It's okay, go get your things. I'll keep an eye on them for a second," a voice emerges from outside the screaming match now on full swing between my kids, and there's Kenna, the young woman I'd met in line, taking a napkin to clean up the sugar mess on the table and talking to the kids.

"Eli? You have such a beautiful drawing, what is it?" she asks, and their eyes fly to her simultaneously. She is smiling and his eyes shyly move down to the drawing in front of him.

"The sea. I want to paint a fishy. Yellow."

"Wow, a yellow fish?" He nods. Her soothing voice is working wonders and both kids are now just calmly looking at her.

"That's a good idea. Wanna hear another good idea?"

He nods again and his eyes slowly go back to her again, eager to discover whatever might come next.

"While Maggie uses the yellow, we can do a green fishy to be yellow fishy's friend. How about that?"

His eyes widen in wonder and his little hand immediately grabs for the green crayon.

"What about me?" Maggie asks shyly.

"Your drawing is beautiful too. What is it? Can you tell me?"

"It's a princess castle. I need the yellow to paint it because we have no golden, so this is the gold. Princesses have golden palaces," she states proudly.

"They do. Their castles also have a lot of pinks and purples, so maybe we could use those too?"

Dropping the yellow, she makes a grab for the pink crayon, and in less than a minute, the coveted crayon now sits abandoned on the table and both kids are happy again. It's like I just witnessed real magic happening in front of me.

"Thank you," I say, and I go grab my order. When I come back to the table, they are still calm and quiet, painting away.

Eli sees me and grabs for his cake pop.

Maggie looks at me and I set her cake pop and smoothie in front of her. She smiles at me grateful and goes back to painting after a sip on the smoothie and a cake pop.

"I appreciate this so much," I mumble, not knowing exactly what to say. She's been a lifesaver, really.

"Don't worry about it, really."

"Let me buy you another coffee?" I offer, thinking that throwing money at a situation usually helps, but she shakes her head.

"No, thanks, can't have too much caffeine or I'll be bouncing off the walls."

"Please, I have to do something," I insist.

Kenna bites her lip, giving me another crooked smile. "Maybe a cake pop?"

"A cake pop?"

"Maybe I have a little problem with sugar," she says, holding up her fingers to indicate a small amount.

I laugh and leave her again with the kids at the table while I go and order her cake pop, bringing it back for her.

She sticks it into her mouth immediately, smiling.

"On the way to school?" she asks after taking a bite.

"No, not yet. Maggie starts the next semester," I explain. "We're off to daycare."

"Oh, which do you use?"

I look at her. "Why do you ask? You can't have kids at your age."

That probably isn't the right thing to say to a total stranger, but she doesn't balk at the question, she actually blushes a little.

"No, no kids yet. I'm just looking for a job."

"Oh?" I ask, raising an eyebrow. "What kind of work do you do?"

She's looking down at Eli when she answers. "I'm taking a gap year for college, but I'm in early education. I just want to work around kids."

This is probably not the best way to find a nanny, but it's

not like I have any prospects currently and I'd just witnessed her averting a major crisis with hardly a hair out of place or dropping her smile once.

"Have you thought about becoming a nanny?" I ask.

"Why? Do you know someone?" she asks, and I look down at my kids with a wry look on my face. She laughs, covering her mouth with her hand. "I'm so sorry; I should have realized."

I shake my head. "Listen, I know this is weird and you don't know me, but you've been great with my kids and I'm looking for someone – if I give you my business card will you email me your resume?"

She looks at me curiously. "Really?"

I reach into my wallet and hand her a business card. "Really. I'd love to interview you."

Kenna gives me a soft smile and takes the business card. "Thank you. Really, I'll send it right away."

She walks toward the bathroom and I wonder if I fucked that completely up with my lack of social graces.

The kids have busied themselves with food and drink and painting and I smile at them, finally feeling like we're settled for the first time this morning. I already had to deal with Maggie having a tantrum because she couldn't find her pink shoes. She starts school next year because she has a late birthday, and so I have her and Eli full-time until then.

I've been a single dad for three years, and it doesn't get any easier, but it also is rewarding. My kids love me and I'd die for them, so I'm happy.

Right?

It's just that sometimes I feel like I'm drowning and I'm all alone, and it's hard. How do you explain to the kids that their mother just left? They need a mother figure in their life. They might not have a lot of memories of her, though

Maggie might, since she had just turned three at the time, but that doesn't mean I'm enough.

And sometimes I just wish I had someone to help me get through the rougher patches. These kids are amazing, yes, but I struggle a lot and I miss having a helping hand. Not that Suzanna ever was one, but it would be nice to have someone to help me along the way, I think.

The kids are good while I drink my coffee and I'm grateful. I've been feeling overwhelmed lately.

Kenna happens to be walking out of the café at the same time that we are. Eli has chocolate from the cake pop all over his face and hands so I'm trying to keep him from wiping it on my suit as I wrangle him into the car seat.

"Kenna is here," Maggie says quietly, and I look up at her.

"I'll shoot you that resume," she says confidently, and gives me a bright smile.

Maybe there's a light at the end of the tunnel.

2

KENNA

I smile as I get into my car, watching the handsome man who's given me his business card and asked me to send a resume pull out of the café parking lot.

How lucky am I to get a job interview at a coffee shop on my first day home? I have to start looking for housing and a job, and this could potentially have both.

Derek Ledderman, Marketing Executive, is all the card says, with a phone number and an email address in the bottom left corner. It's simple, but he was very well dressed and put together, so I assume he has money, though that is mostly irrelevant to me. I just want the experience so that I can put it on a resume and maybe it'll help me get a job in early education once I graduate.

I've only got one semester left, but I've been dealing with burnout from all my extra-curricular activities, and I've had virtually no social life outside of my best friend and room-mate, Cherie. She's great, but she's not exactly the be all and end all to college.

Though this is my first day back home, I've been out of school for a month now, taking the time to just relax and enjoy some down time before I came back, and I haven't made any strides with my social life, but I hope that this is a step in the right direction for my career.

I get home and fix up my resume, adding the experience I had in college, teaching elementary school kids creative writing. I email it right away, writing out a cover letter stating how much I love children and that I'm an eldest sister of two siblings so I've been helping with them since they were born.

After I hit send, I stare at my open email account for far too long before my brother knocks on the door jamb.

"Kenna? Are you coming down to breakfast?"

"I had a cake pop at the café," I explain, and he tilts his head.

"But there's sausage," he says, as if that alone is reason to indulge in a second or even third breakfast. He's a big guy, towering over me even though he's four years younger, and he loves his breakfast meats.

I smile. "Maybe I'll come down and grab at least some sausage," I tell him.

He nods, smiling, and walks downstairs. I follow him, thinking I don't have much else to do. Cherie is still back at college, and I'm staying with my parents, at least until I find a place.

If this works out with Derek Ledderman, I hope it's a live-in position, so that I'll have a job *and* a place to stay that's not here at my parents'.

"How was your morning, Kenna?" my mother asks, kissing my father's cheek as she hands him his coffee. My mother is a homemaker and a stay-at-home mom, and she always has been.

"My sister is in the news again," my father says dryly before I can answer, and I blink at him.

My mother takes in a deep breath.

"What is it this time?" she asks tightly.

My aunt is always in some kind of trouble or other, even when they were younger. "She's getting married," my father says, showing her the paper, and my mother frowns.

"You'd thought she'd learned her lesson the first time," she grumbles. "But I see she's back in town, so we'll see how she handles everything."

"Doesn't her husband still live here?" Ryan asks, his mouth full.

"Chew and swallow before speaking," my mother warns and he does.

"As far as I know," my father answers tightly.

I swallow hard. This is a sore subject for my father. He had always defended his younger sister, as long as I could remember, but in the past few years they'd grown estranged. My father could never understand why she would leave town and leave her husband and family for no other reason than she just wanted to.

Wanting to bring things to a lighter mood, I tell my parents about my potential job offer this morning. Maybe that'll be a good distraction from my aunt.

"We met at the café and his kids were so cute. I hope the interview goes well," I say, and my mother smiles at me, sitting next to my dad.

"At the café? You want to be a barista?" my brother asks and my little sister snickers.

Ugh, siblings. I roll my eyes at them. I love my siblings dearly but sometimes they can be irritating.

"No, it's for a nanny position."

"Oh, wow, right up your alley," my father muses, putting his newspaper down.

I grin back at my family. It feels good to have their

support, even if they are a little worried about me taking a gap year.

"I sent him my resume, now I just have to wait for him to call," I say.

"I'm sure he will," my mother says. "What does he do?"

"Some kind of marketing executive," I say.

Something flashes across my mother's face almost imperceptibly. "I guess there's a lot of those in Los Angeles," she murmurs.

My father looks at her.

I frown, not understanding the look that passes between them, and I reach into my pocket to pull out the business card.

"See? It's a legitimate business card," I argue.

I slide it across to my father and he takes in a deep breath when he looks at it.

"He only talked to you about the job?" he asks.

"Yeah? What else would he talk to me about?" I ask.

"You don't remember him?" my mother asks softly. "You met him a few years ago, at your cousin's third birthday party."

I blink at them, not sure what they mean, but slowly it dawns on me. I swallow hard.

"He's my ex-brother-in-law," my father says softly, and I remember, suddenly, the half-smile that he gave me this morning seeming awfully familiar.

The memory of that afternoon floods me.

"I'm Derek," he'd said, and I'd been staring into his green eyes, already a bit enamored.

Was it weird to have a crush on your uncle? Probably, but I was only eighteen and he was the first extremely attractive man that I'd ever been around.

Even then, he'd had a few gray streaks around his temples, but his smile was warm and inviting.

"N-nice to meet you," I stuttered, and I tried my best not to stare at him the rest of the visit.

He took pictures when I played peek-a-boo with the baby and I blushed.

"Come back to visit soon," he said. "Magpie loves you."

Oh shit. Maggie. I should have known, but I hadn't seen her since she was just out of diapers. My aunt, Suzanna, had left Derek, my would-be employer, and her kids shortly after and disappeared off the map.

I'm never going to get this job.

3

———

DEREK

I receive the email with Kenna's resume quickly, and I smile at my email. That is, until I look at the resume.

It's not that it isn't impressive. She's had experience in college working at small daycares and also with teaching, and she states that she has two younger siblings, so she's had lifelong experience with kids.

That's not the problem.

The problem is her last name. *Lodge.* As in *Suzanna Lodge*, my ex-wife. It dawns on me slowly that Kenna's pretty smile looked familiar.

She'd only been eighteen the last time I saw her, and she'd changed quite a bit since then, her hair longer and a bit darker, gained some weight. But she still has that same smile, and I can't believe that I didn't realize it sooner.

McKenna Lodge is my ex-wife's niece.

I let out a long breath, wondering how much she has in common with her aunt. I can't judge her based on the decisions of one of her family members, can I?

She'd been so good with the kids, and so helpful. I really

16

need a nanny, but do I want to invite someone connected with their absent mother into my home?

This is something I need to sleep on.

I sleep on it, in fact, for six days, and on the seventh day, Eli's screaming bloody murder because I didn't have his Mickey Mouse pajamas clean and Maggie is throwing up in a wastebasket because she ate ten peanut butter cups when I was in the bathroom.

I simply can't do this alone anymore. I need help, and McKenna Lodge may be the person to provide it. I decide to call her and at least give her an interview.

When she answers, Eli's still screeching but Maggie is feeling better, at least.

"Mr. Ledderman?" she answers, sounding surprised.

"Ms. Lodge," I say dryly. "I'm sorry that I didn't recognize you."

"No, no, that's all right. I was young and I didn't recognize you either. I can understand if given what happened with my aunt, you don't want to consider me for the position..." she trails off.

I take in a deep breath. "I can't judge you based on her decisions," I say finally. "You're not her, right?"

"Absolutely not," Kenna says quickly. "In fact, I don't even speak to her. I haven't seen her in years."

I let out the breath that I'd been holding. "Good," I mutter dumbly. I don't know how to handle this situation but I know that I need someone like Kenna to keep from tearing my hair out, so I don't really have a choice. "Are you available to interview this afternoon?"

"Really?" she asks, and then pauses. "Would two work for you?"

"Perfect," I say. I've already taken the day off work since Maggie got sick, so I have all day with them here by myself. I can use her on a day like today, so we'll see how she handles the kids when they're cranky and ill.

I fall asleep on the couch with Eli sucking his thumb in my lap and Maggie lying across my legs. I know I should try and break him of the habit but it's hard to do by myself, and without his mother...

The doorbell rings and I startle awake. Eli starts to whine and holds on to me tightly. I'm able to wrangle out from underneath Maggie without waking her, but Eli's wide awake when I go to the door.

"Hello," Kenna says, smiling at Eli, and he blushes, smiling, and turns his face into my neck.

"He has a bit of a crush, I'm afraid," I say dryly, and Kenna laughs.

"That's very flattering. He's a handsome boy."

"I remember you," he says, still hiding. "From the cake pop store."

Kenna laughs again. "Yes, the cake pop store."

I'm surprised that he remembers since that was a week ago, which is sometimes years in a kid's brain.

Eli won't let me put him down without whining so I hold him as I sit down on the couch.

Kenna sits across from me so as to not disturb Maggie.

"She's sick today," I explain. "Too many peanut butter cups."

Kenna doesn't judge me, just keeps a smile on her face. "Kids will be kids," she says.

I shift Eli to one side so that I can see her better and he stares at her with wide green eyes, his thumb still in his mouth.

"Your resume really speaks for itself," I say. "But I just wanted you to be here when the kids aren't at their best, to see what it's really like."

"They were just a little rambunctious at the café," she admits.

I nod. "They're always at least a little rambunctious. I have trouble keeping childcare for them," I confess.

"That's not on the kids, it's on the professional. We are the adults, we should be able to woo them into behaving and sometimes people just don't want the hassle of connecting to the kids," she commiserates, and I smile back at her, feeling a little bit surprised. I'd never thought of it that way, but I can see her point.

She keeps looking around at the house as if in awe. It's a big house, more like a mansion, because I'd wanted to have a lot more kids than just two. Suzanna couldn't even handle the two we had, though, so it ended up just being me and the kids bouncing around in this big house.

Eli slowly climbs down from my lap and goes over to the corner, where his toys are upturned and spilling out. The housekeeper manages to keep the house mostly clean, but she's off today and so it's a bit of a mess. I probably should have straightened up before inviting Kenna for an interview.

He picks up his toy train and brings it over to the coffee table, pushing it around and making "choo-choo" noises.

"Do you like my train?" he asks. He has trouble with "r" sounds so it comes out like "twain."

"I love trains," Kenna says, and then she kneels down to get to Eli's level, watching him push the train around on the table. "Have you ever been on one?"

"No. I wanna be the 'ductor," he says.

"The conductor? They're very important," Kenna says easily. "Do you have another train so we can play together?"

"Only the caboose," he says, and hurries over to grab it and bring it back to her. I watch as she pushes around the trains, crashing them to make Eli giggle, and I make my decision right then and there.

"I want to hire you," I say, and Kenna looks up from the trains, her eyes widening. "You do? Didn't you have any interview questions?"

"Just one," I say. "When can you move in?"

Kenna grins, standing up, and I stand too, shaking her hand. It feels so small in mine. She really *is* young, but she's wonderful with Eli, and Maggie seems to like her, too.

"Immediately," she answers.

"I can give you a tour right now," I say, but then Maggie wakes up and looks green around the gills, so I grab her up and take her to the bathroom.

Eli usually trails along behind me everywhere that I go, but once Maggie seems to have rid herself of all the peanut butter cups she stole from the pantry, I peek my head back into the living room and Eli's still playing trains with Kenna, who has sat down on the floor with him.

"I will pay you a huge bonus if you can start today," I plead, thinking about all the meetings I have to reschedule and the paperwork I need to finish.

"You don't have to give me a bonus," she says.

"Five grand," I offer, and Kenna blinks at me.

"O-okay," she stutters.

"I'll have my lawyer draw up some paperwork and get it to you by this afternoon, but I'll pay you the five grand in cash," I explain.

She blinks at me again. "Sh-sure, that's fine. Thank you so much for the opportunity, Mr. Ledderman."

"Call me Derek," I say, and Kenna smiles.

"Then call me Kenna."

I deposit Eli and Maggie on the couch and Maggie looks up at Kenna with some interest.

"Kids, this is Kenna. She's going to be your nanny," I explain, worried that Maggie will have a tantrum about it. She had with the last nanny, who had been an older woman that was a little too harsh with the kids. I'm sure she's a nice enough woman, but I don't want anyone who will punish a child for crying after skinning their knees.

Eli grins. "She gets to sleep over?"

I nod. "Most nights." I turn to Kenna. "You can do what you'd like with your weekends, I just work Monday through Friday. I can work at home on weekends."

Maggie is looking at Kenna coolly and I'm a little nervous. Maggie is precocious and she can have a bit of an attitude problem.

"Can we watch Paw Patrol?" Maggie asks, surprising me by looking right at Kenna.

Kenna looks at me and I nod slightly. "Sure thing. When your Dad and I get back, I'll introduce myself more properly, okay?"

Maggie grabs the remote and turns on the show and I let out a long breath.

"I thought she was going to have a bigger reaction," I explain as I lead Kenna up the staircase.

"Lots of times, kids surprise us," she says. "I have to tell you what a beautiful home you have."

I smile. "Thank you. I know it's a bit messy. The housekeeper only comes on Fridays."

"Are you sure it's all right for me to move in right away?"

"It would help me *immensely*," I tell her. "I've had to take so much time off work because the daycare didn't work out. Eli for some reason hated the wallpaper because it had clowns on it."

Kenna shudders. "No wonder, clowns are scary."

I laugh and lead her to the guest bedroom, next to Eli's

room. My bedroom is on the other side, beside Maggie's room.

"Eli often climbs into my bed or Maggie's, so if you can't find him in his room, he'll be with one of us," I explain, opening the doors to the kids' rooms to show her before leading her to her room. I point down the hall. "That's the master bedroom, my room."

Kenna just nods and her blue eyes widen as she looks into the guest bedroom and the four-poster bed. "This is almost bigger than my college dorm room," she says in awe, and I chuckle.

"We can talk about your salary now, if you'd like," I say, and Kenna clears her throat.

"To be honest with you Mr. Ledd—I mean, Derek, I haven't thought much about salary."

I nod. "I'll have my lawyer write something up for tonight. Excuse me for just a moment."

I stride to my bedroom and open up the safe, taking five thousand in cash out to hand to her. Kenna looks overwhelmed, and I'm not surprised. This has all gone pretty quickly, but I have work I need to catch up on, and the kids like her. I have to try *something*.

"I'm free today to watch them but I'll have to go home and grab some of my things for the rest of the week," Kenna says hesitantly.

I smack my forehead. "Of course. I'm sorry to put you on the spot, if you'd like to come back tomorrow—"

She shakes her head and smiles. "It's okay."

Kenna really *does* have a pretty smile. I look away, feeling my cheeks flush. This has all been work-related, business in a way, but when it turns more social, I start getting awkward. This is my cue to go.

"I'll be home at six," I tell her. "Please feel free to make anything out of the fridge."

"Do the kids have a schedule for eating dinner or snacks?" Kenna asks, and I blink at her.

"Uh...not exactly," I say, rubbing the back of my neck. Ever since Suzanna left, I've just kind of been winging it, but I don't want to say that to her.

Kenna doesn't seem perturbed. "That's fine. We'll figure it out," she says easily.

I pause in the doorway of the guest bedroom. "Thank you, Kenna," I say quietly, looking into her blue eyes, and I see the color flush to her cheeks.

"Thank you, Derek, for the opportunity," she says just as quietly, and suddenly everything seems intense and I feel awkward again.

I kiss the kids goodbye, and for once, they don't even cry that I'm leaving.

"Be good for Ms. Kenna, okay?"

They're focused on Paw Patrol and don't answer, so I reluctantly leave the house, letting out a long breath.

It feels like there's a weight lifted off my shoulders. Despite her being related to my ex, Kenna Lodge may just be a godsend.

4

———

KENNA

The way Derek had looked at me right before he left still had me flustered. I definitely shouldn't be thinking about how attractive he is, how his green eyes crinkle at the corners when he smiles. Maybe I still have a little school girl crush on him, or something.

That will change, now that he's my employer.

Right?

I shake my head to clear it and walk back downstairs, where Derek has already left. The house seems so big and empty with just the sounds of the cartoon the kids are watching bouncing off the walls in a weird kind of echo.

I sigh and sit down on the couch between the kids and Maggie looks up at me.

"I puked today," she says, apropos of nothing, and I stare at her for a moment before nodding.

"Your dad told me," I say. "I'm sorry about that. Do you feel better now?"

"A little," she says. "But I still need my doll."

"Your doll?"

"Her name is Melinda. She's upstairs, but I'm tired from all the puking," Maggie says, shifting to lie on the couch.

"Does Melinda make you feel better when you're sick?"

Eli giggles at something on the television, ignoring both of us.

Maggie just looks at me as if I should already know that's the case and I smile at her.

"I'll go get her from your room. What does she look like?"

"She's the only doll that is a baby," she says, sounding exhausted.

I trek upstairs after a moment, looking around at the pictures in the hallway. There are a few with my aunt in them, no wedding pictures, just some of her and the kids, but they make me wince nonetheless.

I thought for sure that I wouldn't get the position after I figured out who Derek was and how I know him but I'm grateful that he gave me the chance.

The kids are really cute, and this is what I need for my resume.

Plus, it'll get me out of my parents' house and I won't have to share a bathroom with my siblings anymore. A win-win situation, really.

Not to mention, this place is *beautiful*. I wish I had asked Derek about taking the kids out to the pool, because it's a huge, Olympic sized one and I'd love to have gotten a few laps in. Not that I brought my swimsuit, so it's probably for the best.

I slip past the guest bedroom (my bedroom now, I suppose), and Eli's room, and walk into Maggie's. There's purple paint all over the walls, purple curtains, purple unicorn posters on the wall. Kid really likes purple, I suppose.

I find Melinda lying on top of her head in a corner and hurry back downstairs, but not before I find a worn polaroid of Maggie as a baby with my aunt holding her. It's lying on Maggie's bedside table. I feel a sting of empathy for the little girl. Despite how my aunt had left them, of course she would still miss her mother.

I clear my throat, not moving the polaroid from where it is, and walk back downstairs with Melinda.

Maggie takes her and hugs her close.

"Do you have a doll or a stuffed animal that makes you feel better when you're sick, Eli?" I ask, and he looks at me, tilting his head as if thinking.

"No," he says. "Just my trains."

"Trains can make you feel better, too," I say, and Eli favors me with a toothy smile. "Do you kids want a snack?" I ask, and Eli nods eagerly.

"I don't know," Maggie hedges. "I don't want to puke again. It's gross."

I wrinkle my nose. "It is gross. So how about some crackers and ginger ale?"

Maggie sits up, seeming a little less listless. "Okay," she says simply, and I feel like I've made some small stride toward getting her to trust me.

Eli is easy, he's young enough that he'll accept new people into his life, but Maggie definitely has her reservations, and I understand why.

"Cheese crackers," Eli pipes up, and I laugh.

"Cheese crackers for Eli," I say in a singsong voice kids usually like. "Do you want to help me make them?"

Eli's green eyes widen. "I can help? Daddy never lets me help," he says excitedly.

"I think we can work something out. Will you be okay here for a moment, Maggie?" I ask.

She waves a hand dismissively and turns the channel to some show about horses and unicorns. I'm not going to win her over in a day, that's for sure.

Eli follows me to the kitchen, and I set up a chair for him to stand on. I take out some shredded cheese from the fridge and crackers from the pantry.

Eli starts eating the cheese, but I've learned in early education to pick my battles, so I let him have a couple of tiny handfuls before I take it from him.

"Spread the crackers around on the plate," I tell him, and he does so, fumbling a little and spilling some.

He looks down at the floor, dismayed. "I made a mess."

I chuckle. "That's okay. We all make messes. We'll clean it up after we're done," I say easily and he gives me another sweet smile.

He looks so much like his father it's almost eerie, especially when he smiles.

I let Eli press the button for one minute on the microwave and he bounces around excitedly until it's done.

"They're hot," I say. "Don't touch."

He nods solemnly and puts his hands behind his back. I pick him up and put him on the floor and take the plate of crackers, carrying the box under my arm and a can of ginger ale in my other hand.

Maggie eats a few crackers and drinks her ginger ale before she conks out again. I guess that being sick that morning really tired her out. Eli and I play trains and watch television, and time goes by so quickly I don't even think about eating myself.

I'm surprised when Derek opens the door, not realizing that so much time has passed.

I haven't even cleaned up the spilled crackers, so I stand up and smile sheepishly.

"I made a bit of a mess in the kitchen," I say. "I'll clean it up."

Derek looks around at Maggie, who's woken up and is coloring on the floor while Eli and I put together a train track, and he offers me a big smile.

It lights up his whole face and makes him look ten years younger, and I feel myself blushing.

I feel kind of bad that he paid me five grand for just a few hours, but Derek looks happy and picks up Eli to give him a kiss on the cheek.

"How you feeling, Magpie?" he asks, and Maggie gives him a little smile.

"Crackers and ginger ale made me feel better," she says, and that's the most glowing recommendation I could have hoped from her.

"I made cheese crackers. In the microwave!" Eli says excitedly, and Derek chuckles.

"I know it's not the healthiest snack," I say hesitantly, but Derek shakes his head.

"You did well, Kenna. Thank you so much. I was able to get a lot of work done, and I appreciate you staying on such short notice."

He pulls out his wallet and hands me two hundred-dollar bills, but I shake my head.

"You've already given me so much," I start.

"No, please take it. You deserve it," he says. "Usually by now the nanny would have already quit, but you have a way with them."

I take the money reluctantly. How much does he *make*? Derek reaches into his briefcase and hands me a multi-page contract. "The contract extends just for six months, just in case you end up finding something else," he explains. "I hope you find the salary to be decent."

My eyes bulge out of my sockets when I see how many zeroes my six month salary has. "Are...are you sure?"

He smiles. "You do good work, and I pay for good work."

"Th-thank you," I stutter, not knowing what else to say.

"Do you need some help moving?" he asks, and I shake my head, not wanting to put him out.

"I just have clothes and a few things," I admit. "I should be moved in by tomorrow."

Derek nods with Eli on his hip.

"Does Kenna come back tomorrow?" Eli asks hopefully, hiding his face in his dad's chest.

Derek pats the little boy's back. "She'll be here every day for a while, buddy."

"Sleeping over?" Maggie asks from the couch, and I think I hear a hopeful tint to her voice, as well.

I can't help smiling. Everything is turning up Kenna, and it feels nice.

5

───────

DEREK

Kenna gets all moved in the next day, and the rest of the week goes by in a blissful blur. I'm able to get plenty of work done and spend time with the kids after work, because Kenna always disappears into her room after I get home.

It's perfect. It's exactly what I wanted, and Kenna doesn't try to make too much conversation and make me feel anxious and awkward. She does her job and she's wonderful with the kids and it's everything I could have hoped for.

There's only one small problem. Miniscule, really.

I find myself more and more attracted to Kenna Lodge.

She's a beautiful young woman, too young for me, really, and there's the little problem that she's my employee and my ex-wife's niece. There's no way that I should be attracted to her, but I am.

It started on the second day, when Eli woke up and barreled into her room, asking her to play with his trains. She got up, yawning, her blonde hair mussed from sleep, blue eyes glassy. She was wearing a pair of yoga shorts and a tank top and I could see her nipples through the thin fabric.

30

I looked away almost immediately, but I've been thinking about it ever since. I can't stop looking at the line of her ass and thighs in the shorts she wears around the house in the summer, but I can't very well tell her what to wear. It isn't anything inappropriate, and she'd been caught off guard the other day.

It isn't like I can complain that a beautiful woman, who's great with my kids, wears shorts around my house, which is also *her* house, at least for the duration of her contract.

I'm thinking more and more that this could be a long-term, permanent thing, if Kenna's interested. I'm willing to offer her more money, more time off, anything she wants. I just have to keep my dirty old man eyes in my eye sockets.

It's disgusting, really. How old can she even be? Twenty? Twenty-two?

I'll be thirty-nine in December, and I can't be going after young girls. It has to be that I haven't been with a woman since Suzanna. I'd tried to turn off that part of myself, tried to lock it away, because falling in love certainly hasn't done me any favors.

There's just something about the way Kenna looked that day, fresh out of sleep, that does it for me. I just need to keep my head down and treat this like a professional relationship.

Friday, her last day before her two days off, Kenna wakes up early and makes breakfast for everyone. The kids are still fast asleep, but I smell bacon and follow the scent downstairs. I don't get many home-cooked meals, usually opting to eat out or worse, eat some of the kids' food like dino chicken nuggets and fries. As a single parent, you eat what you can, when you can. At least that's always been my philosophy.

The one meal of the day the kids don't complain about ever is breakfast, and Kenna's already figured out that Eli loves his waffles and Maggie loves bacon and scrambled eggs with cheese. She knows so much about them already, and I can't ask for a better nanny. They already love her and they've been anxious about her leaving this weekend.

"She goes away tomorrow?" Eli asked with a big pout and wet eyes.

"Not goes away," I say comfortingly. "She's just going to have a couple of days off."

"When is my day off?" Maggie asks, and I snicker.

"Day off from what? Being sassy?"

"I'm a hard worker, Dad," she says with no small amount of attitude, and I smile at her.

"I know, honey," I humor her as she takes one of my briefcases up to her room.

Kenna was in bed at the time and I didn't know exactly how to comfort the kids about her leaving.

I think I'll ask her about it today.

The kids don't usually get up until seven, unless I wake them up early, and it's only six, so I've got time to chat with her.

When I walk downstairs, I see her in the kitchen, humming along to some song on the radio and shaking her hips, and I clear my throat, trying not to watch her.

"Oh!" she says, flustered and putting down the spatula in her hand. "Sorry, I hope it's okay to use your kitchen—"

"You can use it anytime you like, you know that," I say easily. "But you don't have to make a full breakfast every morning."

She flushes, turning to look at me with wide blue eyes. "But I want to give back, somehow. You've done so much for me, Derek."

I look at her only for a moment before looking away again, my cheeks heating up. I'm so *bad* at this, the social interactions that come from small talk, but I can make this business, and that'll help.

"I need to talk to you about something," I say, and Kenna turns off the stovetop.

"I'm finished anyway," she says, turning around and wiping her hands on a towel before tossing it on the counter. "Would you like me to make you a plate?"

I shake my head. "I'll make it myself."

"I've already got it ready," she complains. "And I made coffee. I've finally figured out your crazy coffee machine."

I laugh. "All right, then," I say awkwardly, sitting down at the table.

She makes me a plate and brings it to me with my coffee, lots of cream and sugar. I guess she's figured out how I like my coffee after spending a week here.

"Thank you," I murmur, and Kenna smiles, sitting across from me at the dining table with her own plate.

"What did you need to talk to me about?" she asks.

I sigh. "The kids are asking why you have days off, and I think they're just getting really used to having you around all the time. Maggie seems okay with it, but Eli's getting really attached."

Kenna frowns. "Is that a bad thing?"

I think about it for a moment and tilt my head. "I don't know. After their mother left, I don't want them to have to go through that hurt of being abandoned again. And so far it's been okay, because most nannies don't last longer than a day or two, but..." I trail off.

"But I've been here a week and you are afraid of them getting attached and me leaving them one day out of the blue," she says quietly.

I look up at her, surprised at her insight on the matter. "Exactly. It's kind of tricky."

"It is," she nods. "But at the same time, I think him being attached to me isn't a bad thing. I'm going to be his nanny for at least six months."

I clear my throat again. "About that...would you be willing to extend your contract? Things have been going so well and I could boost your pay—"

"Oh, God, no," she says, and I'm stricken for a moment before she waves her hands, shaking her head. "I mean, not no to extending the contract. No to more money. You pay me way more than enough."

"Still, if I can help your transition back to school—"

"It's only one semester," she says with an even smile. "I'll figure it out. Don't worry. This is a dream job for me, really, so I'm not going anywhere."

I let out a relieved breath. "Thank God, because, Kenna, you've really been a miracle around here."

I'm telling the truth. The kids are on a better schedule with eating and activities, bedtimes and wakeups are going way more smoothly, and the most important thing is that they're *happy*. Even Maggie, who has the tendency to push people away, hasn't done that to Kenna.

Kenna blushes and looks away. "I'm really glad. I think they're amazing kids, and you're an amazing father, Derek."

I smile back at her, even though she's not looking at me, and start to eat my food.

"This is amazing, Kenna. Maybe you should also be my personal chef," I tease, and Kenna laughs, surprised.

"Is that a joke?"

"I think so," I say, chuckling. "I do have a few of them."

"It's nice to hear you laugh," she says softly, and I look up at her, meeting her bright blue eyes. My throat goes tight, my heart beating faster.

Stop it, Derek, I tell myself. *She's too young for you.*

Kenna stands up to put her plate in the sink. "Should I go and wake the kids?" she asks, but my body isn't listening to my brain and I stand up, walking up behind her at the sink.

"Not yet," I murmur, reaching around her to grab a glass, telling myself it's just to pour some orange juice and not because I want to touch her.

She takes in a little gasping breath as I reach around her, my forearm brushing against her hip. Kenna turns and looks up at me, her chin tilted up just slightly, and it's like I completely lose my mind.

I lean down and kiss her, delving my tongue into her mouth to slide it against hers, and Kenna makes this little surprised moan into my mouth, leaning into me.

That's when the kids thunder down the stairs.

"I smell bacon!" Maggie yells, and I break apart from Kenna suddenly, stalking back over to the table to grab my suit jacket off the back of the chair.

"Gotta go to work," I mutter, and kiss the kids goodbye as quickly as I can.

I run out of there like the house is on fire.

What was I *thinking?* I've got to keep it together, no matter how attractive Kenna Lodge is.

She's my kids' nanny, my employee, and in her early twenties. I can't go down that road for so many reasons.

6

KENNA

I can't believe that Derek kissed me, but what I really can't believe is that I kissed him *back*. I know that I have a little bit of a crush on him, but still, I can't kiss my boss! What was I thinking?

It had to have been just a little slip of judgment on his part. He didn't mean it. Right?

My heart beats too hard against my chest plate the rest of the morning, even as the kids eat and chat about everything and nothing. I chat right along with them, trying to forget how their father's mouth felt against mine.

The day goes by in a blur and when Derek arrives, I make my way out of the door quickly after saying goodbye to the kids. Eli pouts and almost cries, but Maggie just hugs me briefly and goes back to playing.

"Everyone gets days off, Eli," she tells him, and he sniffles but takes her hand as they go toward the toy box.

Derek steps outside with me, to my absolute horror, and I can't look up at him. My cheeks are on fire and he'll know that he flustered me this morning...

"Kenna, please forgive me for this morning," he says, almost mournfully, and I look up at him.

"It's no problem," I say easily. "It was a mistake," I say, my heart dropping just a little.

Derek smiles awkwardly. "I'll make an effort to remain professional from now on," he says, and I nod, eager to get to my car and get the hell out of here.

He doesn't say anything more and I'm afraid he'll try to give me more money so I rush off to the car and peel out of there toward my parents' house, breathing hard.

They've been calling, asking how it's going, and I've been telling them it's great. It *has* been great, up until now. And if I'm honest with myself, the kiss was great, too.

He'd kissed me so deep and thoroughly that it'd nearly knocked me off my feet, but that's never going to happen again. He's not interested in me like that, and I just have a little crush, that's all.

Who wouldn't? He's very handsome and sweet, and a great father. Any woman would have trouble living with such a man and not developing a crush. It's definitely not my fault.

I pull up at my parents' with my little overnight bag and my mom hugs me tightly at the door.

"I'm so glad you're home; we've missed you around here," she says.

"I've only been gone a week, Mom," I say dryly, but she kisses my cheek.

"Still. How is your job going?"

"It's wonderful. The kids are great," I say honestly.

"And Derek? He isn't an overbearing boss, is he? He seems to have that vibe."

I shake my head. "No, not at all." And he hasn't been.

He's very professional, which is why I was so surprised when he kissed me.

I'm still surprised, still floored, honestly, but it doesn't matter. It will never happen again. Why does that make my heart sink, though? It's just a crush. I'll get over it.

"That's good to hear. I was afraid he would judge you for what your aunt did," my mother says, ushering me into the house where she's made breakfast. I can smell the bacon in the air and I'm suddenly ravenous.

I'm chowing down on my bacon, eggs, and toast when my mother looks at me curiously.

"Don't you think it'll be hard, having a social life while you live at that big mansion?" she asks.

She and my father had helped me move in my things, and they were both just as awed as I was at the sight of the mansion.

I shrug. "Never had much of a social life before."

My mother sighs. "I know. You haven't made any strides in giving me grandchildren."

I choke on my toast. "Mom, please," I groan.

"I'm serious," she says. "I know that you're still so young, but by the time I was your age—"

"I know, I know. You told me all about how you met Dad and it was love at first sight. You wanted him immediately, so you went after him. Dad was shy and reserved and you had to fight to get him to realize that you were interested in him. A year later, you guys were married and I was on the way."

She sighs, smiling. Maybe even reliving a few of those moments for a second or two. "I'm just saying, honey. Keep your heart open," she pleads.

"It's open," I insist, shoveling more food into my mouth. My mother's breakfast is one of the only things I miss about living here. "I just want to focus on my career for now."

"And you're doing great, sweetie," my mother praises. "Just don't forget to have a little fun, too, okay?"

I smile at her after swallowing my food. "Thanks, Mom. I'll try."

"That's all I ask."

She busies herself with cleaning up since my brother and sister have already eaten and went off to school. We're alone in the house and I'm not quite sure how to fill up the awkward silence, at least not without talking about grand-kids, so I go up to my room.

I lie down on the bed and look up at the ceiling. All I can think about is Derek's mouth, the way he'd slid his tongue against mine. I'm going to go crazy.

I huff out a breath and run myself a hot bath, hoping that the steam will clear my head. I even light myself a candle. I like to go all out when it comes to my own self-care.

I'm not one of those high-maintenance girls, even though I think they're beautiful. I don't wear much makeup or buy designer clothes or anything like that. I do enjoy a good skincare routine and my baths, though, and they're usually relaxing.

I don't feel relaxed when I undress and slip into the water, though. I feel antsy, like something's crawling around under my skin. My skin feels flushed all over and not just from the hot water. My nipples peak above the water and I bite my lip.

It's not like I've never been aroused before, but I have virtually no experience with men. I'd never been kissed before Derek kissed me, unless you count a peck on the cheek, and I certainly don't. I don't even really touch myself. I've never had what amounts to an orgasm, and I wouldn't know how to do it even if I tried.

So, I remain sexually frustrated, especially because I

can't stop thinking about Derek's green eyes, his generous mouth. God, I hope I wasn't a bad kisser.

I hope that isn't our last kiss.

I shake my head, sitting up in the bath. Of course that's going to be our last kiss. There's nothing more to do. It's not like we could *date*. He wouldn't want to. He's not interested in me like that, particularly because I'm related to his ex-wife.

Plus, he's a good deal older than me. He probably thinks of me as some little girl playing house with his kids. The thought depresses me, but in the end, I know it's the right thing to do to push it out of my mind.

I'd kissed him back, after all, and I shouldn't have.

I trail my hand along my breasts, palming over my nipples, and wonder what Derek's mouth would feel like *there*. Or maybe lower, past my hip bone, down to the apex between my legs...

I trail my hand down there, too, and gasp when I slide across the button that I know is meant for pleasure, even though I've never really explored there.

Just as I'm about to touch there again, explore more, someone bangs on the bathroom door.

"Hurry up, my back teeth are floating!" my teenage brother screams, and boom, there goes the mood.

I sigh and get up out of the bathtub, drying off and throwing on a pair of sweats and an old T-shirt of my dad's, and plop back down on the bed with my hair still wet.

This is why I hate living with my parents. Can't even daydream about kissing my boss in peace. Part of me can't wait to go back to Derek's. The other part... well, that part hopes he might kiss me again.

It's a complicated place, my head.

7

DEREK

The weekend goes by somehow too quickly *and* too slowly. I love spending all the time with the kids, particularly because I feel since Kenna moved in, I don't see them as much. That's just because I'm back at work, though, and God knows I need to be back at work.

I definitely don't need to spend any more time at home when Kenna's going to be there. I'm afraid to be alone with her, really. I need to talk to her, to apologize again, but I also don't want to bring it up anymore. I hate that I took advantage of her kind nature, and that isn't like me. I keep work at work and home at home, and I always have.

I don't know what's wrong with me.

Maybe I should listen to Grayson and Loxton when they try to set me up with various women. Maybe it would help and I wouldn't kiss my nanny in the kitchen.

I sigh and heft up a sleeping Eli on one hip. It's Sunday evening and Kenna should be returning any minute.

She uses her key to get in the door as I'm halfway up the stairs taking Eli to bed.

"Let me take him," she says, hurrying up the stairs and

grabbing him from my arms. It feels like an electric tingle when she touches my hand taking him, but I ignore it, smiling at her.

"I let them stay up too late," I admit sheepishly, and Kenna chuckles.

"That's your right as their Dad."

She takes Eli up the stairs and I follow her as she tucks him into bed. He wakes up and smiles at her sleepily.

"Kenna, sing me the song," he says, and I can't stop watching from the doorway.

Kenna looks toward the doorway and I move out of her line of sight, not wanting to embarrass her. She begins to sing in a clear voice, lower than I would have expected.

"You are my sunshine, my only sunshine, you make me happy when skies are gray..."

Her voice is beautiful and I can't help the smile that spreads across my face. I'm exhausted from being up late with the kids and waking up at six this morning because Kenna has the kids on such a good sleep schedule, but it all seems worth it right now.

I've done the right thing, hiring Kenna.

She brushes past me when she leaves Eli's room and she jumps, startled, with her hand on her chest.

"Oh, you scared me," she murmurs, chuckling.

I hold up my hands. "Wasn't my intention." I keep looking at her mouth. I have to stop, so I clear my throat and look away.

Suddenly, words I hadn't planned on saying are leaving me and I have no idea where they even came from. "Do you want a drink?"

Kenna blinks at me, as if surprised. "Yeah. That would actually be nice," she says in a low tone so as not to wake up Eli.

We head downstairs and I'm already kicking myself. I told myself I would keep this professional, and inviting her for a drink isn't exactly professional.

What am I doing?

I just need the smallest amount of liquid courage. Just so I can tell her that I'm sorry and that I won't ever do it again. Sure, I've already told her, but I don't want her to feel awkward here. I don't want to feel awkward, either, thus the wine.

I have a bottle of nineteen eighty-two chardonnay that I've been saving for a special occasion, but I figure it's time to pop it.

Kenna's eyes widen as she picks up the bottle, looking at it. "This has to be a two-thousand-dollar bottle of wine," she whispers.

"I got a good deal on it," I tell her easily, pouring us both a big glass. I gulp at mine but she sips at first before groaning low in the back of her throat.

Something like electricity shoots through me. I'm just wearing a T-shirt and a pair of sweats but I'm hot under the collar like I'm wearing a three-piece suit all of a sudden.

"This is so delicious," she murmurs, gulping more of it down.

I chuckle. "There's plenty. I have two more bottles in the fridge."

"Are you some kind of wine connoisseur?" she asks, and I shake my head.

"Not really. But I have a long-term client who owns a vineyard, and he often gifts me bottles like these."

"It pays to be in advertising," she mutters, looking at the glass of wine as if it's made of magic.

I smile and finish my glass, pouring myself another. I'm

a big guy and one glass isn't going to grease the wheels of my social awkwardness.

"I really appreciate everything you've done for me and the kids," I say earnestly, and Kenna blushes, smiling as she looks away. "I'm serious," I say, searching for her gaze and finally catching it when she looks up.

"I'm grateful for the job," she says. "And the kids, they're so great, Derek. You're such a good father."

It's my turn to blush, but I keep looking at her, not wanting to break eye contact. I want her to know how serious I am. "About the other day—"

She waves a hand dismissively. "Don't mention it, Derek, really. It's fine. Living in close quarters like this, things are bound to pop up."

I hum in the back of my throat in response. "You think so?"

Kenna shrugs. "I mean, we're both adults. We can handle it, right?"

My throat works and I pour myself another glass of wine. "I have to blame myself. I haven't seen anyone else since Suzanna left."

Kenna stares at me. "Wh-what? No one? Didn't she leave—"

"Before Eli started walking," I confirm, and Kenna whistles low under her breath.

"That's a long time," she says.

"Yeah," I laugh softly. "So, I guess I'm just not very good at being around young, beautiful women."

"I'm not that young," Kenna complains. "Or that beautiful."

I bite my lip, looking into her bright blue eyes. "I beg to differ."

She looks nothing like her aunt, who's a natural brunette

with sharp, hazel-colored eyes. They're both beautiful, but Suzanna's beauty had always been slightly cold.

There's nothing cold about Kenna. She's warm and bubbly and exactly what my children have been needing in their lives.

Part of me thinks she's what *I've* been needing, too.

The wine must be going to my head. I turn to put up the wine bottle just as Kenna has picked it up to pour herself another glass, and our fingers brush against each other.

She looks up at me, her mouth open and slightly pouted.

"Derek," she says in a low tone.

"Yes?" I respond, trying not to look at that mouth of hers.

"What if I wanted you to kiss me again?" she leans toward me.

I could say no. I *should* say no and let her down easy, tell her that we have to be professional because of the kids. If I was a good man, that's what I would do.

I'm not a good man.

I tilt my head down just slightly and brush my mouth against hers, not deeply like the other day, but just softly. Kenna moans and leans forward, though, wrapping her arms around my neck, and the wine bottle clatters into the sink. It's probably spilling down the drain, but I couldn't care less.

She presses her mouth against mine, deepening the kiss, and I finally cup her face in my hands and pull her away.

"Kenna, if we don't stop now..." I warn.

"I don't want to stop," she murmurs, and I should stop anyway. I should push her away and tell her that this isn't right, that I'm too old and my heart is too worn, too broken. I should tell her to stop, but instead, I lift her small frame onto the kitchen counter.

She stares at me with her blue eyes half-lidded and I lick my lips when she places her hands on my chest.

There's a lot of things I should be doing right now, but for the first time in a really long time, I'm doing what I want. Not what's best for the kids, not what will protect my heart, not what's best for my career.

Just what I want.

I'm already lost in her bright blue eyes, and I'll deal with the consequences when they come.

8

———

KENNA

We don't make it to the stairs. Derek picks me up, kissing me as he walks to the living room, and he lies me down on the big wraparound couch. He tugs off my shorts and I squeak in surprise but I cannot stop smiling.

This is what I've always wanted. When I thought about my first time, I didn't think about roses and candlelight. I want someone who just cannot *wait* to have me, someone who wants me so bad they can't think straight, and that's exactly what Derek is giving me.

It's perfect.

My heart is hammering against my chest plate but I'm not afraid, just excited. Every touch of his skin makes me feel like I'm going to explode, something pulling in my lower stomach that I've never quite felt before.

Derek takes more time taking off my panties, kissing along my knee and my calf as he pulls them off, and then looking down hungrily between my spread legs. I blush, a little worried because I haven't shaved – I had no idea that a glass of wine would go this way, but I'm glad that I had one, otherwise I'd probably be so nervous I couldn't stand myself.

He doesn't seem to care that I'm unshaven, hooking my knees on his shoulders and pressing his face against my bare sex while I clap my hand over my mouth to keep from crying out.

"You taste so sweet," he murmurs against my inner thigh. "Like honey." I catch his gaze before he dives back in and the flat of his tongue drags across that sensitive spot and my hips buck involuntarily. No one has ever touched me like this before. I haven't even touched *myself* like this before, not really. It all seems like too much and I'm panting after just a few moments, not knowing what to expect.

There's something building in my lower abdomen, making me feel more and more giddy, lightheaded from more than just the wine, and Derek moans against me before lifting his face to look at me.

He sits up on his knees in between my legs and I look down at his crotch, unable to help myself. I've never seen him with his shirt off and suddenly I want to, reaching up and tugging at the hem of it with a pout.

Derek chuckles and takes it off, grabbing it with one hand and pulling it over his head to toss on the floor.

His chest is broad and sprinkled with blond hair. He's clearly a natural blond, not that I had doubted it. His skin is tight all over, a six-pack abdomen that I run my hand across, nearly unable to believe that I'm in this position with such a good-looking man.

He's *gorgeous*, even more so than I had expected.

When his hands drop to the waistband of his sweats, my eyes drop lower, and I can see the thick, hard line of him through his sweats. I have a panicked moment where I wonder how I'm going to fit something that big inside me, but when he pushes down his sweats and releases himself, my mouth goes dry.

He's big, I can tell that even from my lack of experience, and I'm a little afraid at first but he doesn't ram into me or anything like that. He takes himself in hand, biting his lip, and looks down at me.

"You're so tight," he marvels, sliding just one finger inside of me and then two, when I start to loosen up.

"It's, ah, been forever for me, too," I gasp out, hardly able to make words. I don't want to lie to him, but I also don't want him to stop because it's my first time and he might not be okay with that.

Derek hums in the back of his throat and then guides himself into me, achingly slowly. I tense up, expecting it to hurt, but it doesn't. It's a little uncomfortable as he pushes the head of his cock into me, but then he waits, panting, looking down at my face.

"You okay?" he asks in a low murmur, and I nod my head so eagerly it makes me a little dizzy. He gives me this charming half smile that makes my heart stutter and then slowly slides into me, inch by inch.

I'm gasping in breaths and wondering how women have the breath to scream during times like this. It's all I can do to gasp in oxygen with the way my body feels, hot to the touch, sensitive everywhere, and when Derek cups my breasts through my tank top, my nipples peak under his touch, as if wanting more.

I want more. I want him to move but I also am afraid that it will hurt and I'm thinking too much but then...

Derek leans down to kiss me, deep and slow, searching my mouth with his tongue, and I stop thinking so much, let my body take over. I roll my hips up to meet him when he starts to move, and he drags along some spot inside of me that makes black spots appear across my field of vision. That building in my lower abdomen is climbing, climbing like I'm on a rollercoaster.

"You're so fucking beautiful," Derek mutters, groaning low in his chest and I reach up to dig my nails into his shoulders, closing my mouth and making muffled sounds of pleasure as he continues to thrust in and out of me in long, slow strokes.

When I finally reach the peak of my orgasm, my *first* orgasm, I drag my nails down his back and I'm sure I've left marks, but Derek just moans, dropping down to cup my face in his hands, still moving his hips and kissing me over and over until I feel dizzy all over again from lack of oxygen.

After a half dozen more strokes he stills and groans and I can feel him spilling inside me and I want to laugh, suddenly, feeling giddy and wonderful, like I've had half a bottle of champagne. Is this what sex is always like? God, how do people not do it on the street corners, if so?

I can't imagine feeling any better than I do right now. My friends in high school and college had talked about it, of course, but they'd never said it could be like *this*.

Derek shudders against me and kisses me again, sloppy and open mouthed, and I could just kiss him forever but there's goosebumps popping up along my skin.

"You're cold," he murmurs, and slowly pulls out of me.

I can't help letting out a little whine and he smiles again, that half-smile that I've only seen a few times from him. He takes a blanket from the top of the couch and puts it over me, adjusting himself back into his sweats. I hate how cold I feel when he stands up, grabbing for my shorts and panties and I don't want this to be over yet. I watch him with a pout.

Suddenly, his features start changing. His smile fades and his eyes widen slightly. "Shit," he says, pressing a hand to his forehead as if he has a headache. "Shit. I shouldn't have done that," he mutters, mostly to himself, and I sit up, frowning.

"Derek," I start, but then a set of tiny footsteps plods down the large staircase. A sleepy eyed Eli, with his sandy hair all mussed, says, "I had a nightmare," hiccupping out a sob, and Derek hums in the back of his throat and picks him up.

"It's okay, sweetheart," he tells him comfortingly. "I've got you."

Then he leaves me there, still half-naked under the blanket, and takes Eli back upstairs.

My heart is about to beat out of my chest from what just happened and almost getting caught by Eli, and I can't think straight.

What did he mean? He shouldn't have done what?

Me?

God, I hope not. Because I want him to do that again, and as soon as possible. I know that he's my boss. I know that he's a lot older than me and that my aunt broke his heart and ruined his life.

But...what if we're meant to be together? What if it's just like in all the books and the movies? I've always been a romantic at heart, and deep down, I've always dreamed of having a husband and a family.

I'm getting ahead of myself. I just need to talk to him, let him know that everything is okay, but when I get dressed and walk up the stairs, Eli's door is closed.

I knock lightly, but when I get no answer, I push open the door just slightly. Derek's spread out on Eli's twin bed with the little boy lying on his bare chest, and it's a sight that makes my heart ache.

There will be time to talk about this in the morning.

9

———

DEREK

I sneak out of Eli's room at four in the morning, showering and trying to get the scent and feeling of Kenna Lodge off my body. I've lost my goddamned mind.

I just acted. I didn't think about what it would mean to kiss her, to make love to her....

And now I have to pay the price. She could sue me, for god's sake, for sexual harassment. She could tell everyone that I'm a dirty old man who took advantage of her kind nature. My kids could lose someone they've gotten close to all over again, and for what? So I could get my rocks off? Jesus, Eli had almost caught us. How would I have explained that?

I blame the wine, even though I didn't drink nearly enough of it for it to make my thoughts fuzzy, and I blame being celibate for the last three years.

I should have listened to Grayson and dated someone, or to Loxton and at least hooked up with someone. Then maybe I wouldn't be in this predicament. I manage to finish my shower without thinking too much about Kenna, pushing the way she'd looked under me out of my mind, although it's always there, pushing against my other thoughts.

She'd been so soft and sweet and...*gorgeous*.

I'm not even the kind of man to go after younger women. All of my girlfriends have been around my age and I always thought badly of those who chased women ten or twenty years younger than them.

I don't know what is going on with me.

Am I having a mid-life crisis?

I dry off quickly, being as quiet as possible when I slip out into the hall after getting dressed. I'm going to work at an ungodly hour, but that's because I can't imagine what I'll say to Kenna, not after what happened last night.

She'll probably want to quit immediately and call me at work, but at least I can get a couple of hours in.

God, I really fucked all this up.

I sigh and leave a short note: *Gone to work early. Be home by six.* I sign my name and stick it on the refrigerator next to one of Maggie's drawings of a unicorn and a princess.

The kids. That's the worst part about all of this. They really care about Kenna. She's really gotten through to them, even Maggie, and that means something.

I don't know how I'm going to work in this state, but I have to try. God knows how long it'll take to find more childcare after this.

If ever.

I'm surprised to see Grayson in the office already, frowning at his computer. We don't even normally work in the same building, so I narrow my eyes at him.

"You in trouble with the missus or something?" I ask, and Grayson barks out a laugh.

"Not this time. My computer crapped out and I'm waiting for IT to fix it."

"So, you decided to steal one of mine?"

I'm the head of marketing at Grayson's father's company, and I've since partnered with Grayson and own part stock, as well. I'm on the board of directors along with Grayson and his father, and we all work together well. It's one of the reasons Grayson and I have stayed close friends, except for those five years when Lilian was away, while Logan...well, that's a story for another time.

Loxton has even kept up his end of being CEO of his father's textile company, and we've seen less and less of him with his new wife, Sadie. I'm happy for Grayson and Loxton, don't get me wrong, but sometimes, I can't help but feel a little resentful.

They both seem to have found love in unlikely places, but I haven't had that pleasure.

Of course, I'm not looking for it. I haven't looked for it since Suzanna, because the way that went I would never wish upon anyone. At least, unlike Grayson, I didn't miss out on my kids' lives, though. That's something, at least.

"You seen the news yet? I know it was in the paper for the last couple of weeks at least, but since you haven't mentioned yet..." Grayson asks, shrugging as he looks at me curiously, and I snort.

"Who reads the paper? What are you, sixty?"

"Okay, old man," he shoots back. "I'm just trying to give you a heads-up."

"What's been in the paper?" I ask, and Grayson rubs the back of his neck. I stare at him. "Grayson, spit it out."

He sighs and hands me a newspaper, one of the local Los Angeles times.

I flip through it, frowning, not seeing anything I should be concerned about until I see it on the third page.

Suzanna Lodge to be married on April fifteenth at Barrington Church, to her long-term fiancé, Benjamin Baker.

The air goes out of my lungs. I don't feel jealous, like I might have thought, or upset. I mostly feel annoyed.

"So, Suzanna's back in town," I say wryly and throw the paper down on the desk.

Grayson frowns, "Are you okay?"

I roll my shoulders, feeling irritation spread across my body, tensing my muscles. "As long as she stays away from me and my kids, I don't care what the fuck she does."

Okay, so I'm still angry. Who wouldn't be?

"Your ex-wife left town in the middle of the night three years ago and disappeared off the map, and now you're okay with her being back in town?" Grayson asks incredulously.

"I'm not *okay* with it, but I don't care that she's getting married."

When I say it, I realize that it's true. I'm over Suzanna Lodge, and that part of my life is over. She left it all behind when she dropped me and her own kids, and I don't want anything to do with her. It's almost a relief that it doesn't hurt anymore, not like it used to. I thought for a while that maybe she'd broken me forever, and maybe she has.

But at least the sight of her name doesn't devastate me the way it would have a year after she left.

Grayson smiles at me. "I'm glad that you've moved past it, Derek. I really am." He pauses, pecking at a button on the computer. "This system is so different from ours," he grumbles.

"So, quit using it and wait for the IT guy," I say dryly, and Grayson groans.

"I guess." He looks at me for a long moment. "You sure you're okay?"

"Fine," I say evenly, even though I don't really like the idea of her back in town. I don't want Maggie to see her while we're out, so I think I'll keep the kids at home as much as I can. I should tell Kenna....

It won't matter. Kenna will probably want to move out as soon as possible. I feel my shoulders slump, thinking about it.

"Something's definitely going on with you," Grayson says. "You want to go to the Dive tonight?"

"Can't," I say firmly. "Got the kids."

"I heard you got a new nanny," Grayson smirks. "Is she pretty?"

"Don't," I say, my eyes snapping to his.

He holds out his hands. "Sore subject. Okay."

I sigh. "*Not* a sore subject."

It *is* a sore subject, and that's all my fault. I overstepped my boundaries with Kenna and now I don't have a clue what to do about it.

Grayson frowns, standing up and clapping me on the shoulder. "Come on, Derek. You can talk to me."

I groan, looking over at him. "You didn't use to be this helpful before Lilian came back into your life, you know?"

He grins. "I know. She makes me a better man."

I make a mock gagging sound in the back of my throat. "Fine. Take me to breakfast or something, and I'll tell you all about it. It's depressing here this early in the morning."

～

GRAYSON and I go out to a breakfast diner nearby the office. It's a small place with a lot of businessmen, but no one is in there this early. It's only about five-thirty, after all.

"What were you doing in the office so early, anyway?"

He makes a face. "Big merger coming up with these guys from the East Coast. Haven't you been reading the board notes?"

"Not really," I confess. I've missed quite a few board meetings with my childcare situation up in the air. "You know what a mess it's been trying to find someone to watch the kids."

Grayson nods. "I'm lucky that my parents love to watch the kids, and that Lilian and I can pick our schedules. You found a new girl, though, right?"

"Girl is the operative word," I mutter, thinking about how young Kenna is. She hasn't even graduated college.

Grayson raises an eyebrow. "So, a young, *pretty* girl?" He grins.

"That's what has me in trouble," I admit. "I overstepped the boundaries after her first week, and now I don't know what to do."

He chokes on his coffee. "What? Derek, I wasn't serious. I didn't think you would be the type to go after your nanny."

I groan. "I didn't *go* after her. Not really, anyway," I mutter.

"So, what happened?"

"I don't know! One thing led to another, and then Eli almost caught us and I felt like shit about all of it."

Grayson whistles. "That's quite a predicament. I *told* you that you should have let me set you up."

"I know, I know," I mutter, spearing at my bacon and eggs. They're not nearly as good as the breakfast that Kenna makes.

"So... do you... like her?" he asks hesitantly.

I give him a withering look. "No."

I don't. Do I?

I shake my head. "It doesn't matter because it's not like that. It was a temporary lapse of judgment."

He shrugs, sipping his coffee. "So? You're both adults. Tell her it was a mistake. That you want her to keep working there, but you'll stay away from her."

I'm quiet for a moment.

"You *can* stay away from her, right?"

"Of course I can," I snap. "She's not even out of college."

Grayson raises his hands as if in defense. "All right, all right. So, just keep things professional, like you said."

I don't know why Grayson's good advice is making me feel annoyed, but I also can't understand why I did that in the first place.

"Sorry," I mumble. "I'm annoyed with myself, and I'm taking it out on you."

He nods. "I get it. That's what friends are for." He looks up at me from his coffee and pauses. "But, Derek, it might not be the world's worst idea—"

"It is," I say firmly, and Grayson drops it. If it had been Loxton, he wouldn't have, but that's the way Grayson is. He understands where I'm coming from, and we've been close friends forever. Even when we were not that close, I always knew him better than most and he still knew me just the same..

"The kids love her, right?" Grayson says. "Just keep away from her, and tell her that you're sorry that you weren't more professional."

I nod, hoping against hope that I haven't ruined this for my kids. I have to do what Grayson says, and try to salvage things. Hopefully, Kenna will understand.

10

———

KENNA

I'm all pins and needles all day, waiting for Derek to come home. He makes it home at two in the afternoon, which is ridiculously early for him. He usually doesn't pull into the garage until six, sometimes seven in the evening.

I'm holding my breath as the kids run to greet him, Maggie to show him the drawings she and I had done, and Eli because he's had a bit of a rough day, after his nightmare.

The nightmare had been about Eli being alone in a big toy store and unable to find his father or anyone he knew. It sounds a lot like a fear of abandonment dream from my studies in child psychology, but I don't think it's the right time to bring something like that up.

"Hello," I say, and Derek nods at me, unsmiling.

"Hello, Kenna," he says tightly, and he won't quite look at me.

My heart drops into my stomach. What have I done wrong? Was I no good in bed? It had been my first time, so if I wasn't, I thought that would make sense, but—

"Can we talk?" he asks, as soon as we get Eli and Maggie

on the couch and watching their afternoon show, something about a puppy who delivers mail.

I nod, but instead of taking me into the kitchen like I expect, he leads me out onto the balcony on the first floor. There's a gorgeous view of the yard from here, and I've never been out there for fear the kids would follow me and possibly fall.

"Kenna," he starts, and then closes his mouth. He's still not looking at me.

"Derek, it's okay," I say softly. "Whatever you have to talk about, it's okay."

"I don't want you to leave," he bursts out, finally looking up at me, his green eyes searching my face.

I'm taken aback. "I wouldn't do that, Derek. I would never leave Eli and Maggie."

"I mean, because of what happened last night," he mutters, rubbing a hand across the back of his neck.

I stare at him. "Wh-what do you mean?"

"It was a mistake."

"Just like kissing me was a mistake?" I shoot back, unable to help myself.

"You're too young. You're my kids' nanny, for god's sake," Derek mutters, as if to himself.

"I'm twenty-two," I say, and it sounds dumb even to my own ears.

"Jesus." Derek runs a hand through his hair, seeming nervous. "Look, Kenna, I'm really sorry about last night. I promise nothing like that will ever happen again."

What if I want it to? I don't say it, even though I want to. Tears are springing to the backs of my eyes and I just need him to stop talking so that I can hole myself up in my room and pretend none of this ever happened.

"It's fine," I say softly. "Don't worry. It was just a mistake, right?"

Derek reaches for his wallet and I put my hand out.

"I'm not a prostitute," I spit out, and Derek looks stricken.

"That's not...I didn't mean..."

"I know," I breathe out, trying to push down my anger at the way he's trying to pay me off. "Just drop it. It never happened."

I walk back into the living room, forcing myself to smile at Eli when he waves at me, and go upstairs, locking the door behind me and throwing myself on the bed. I cry into my pillow for what seems like two hours, and then finally sit up, brushing tears from my face, when there's a small knock on my door.

"Who is it?"

"Maggie," she says softly. "Daddy said you weren't feeling well. I made you some soup."

I wipe my eyes and go to the door, looking down at Maggie who is holding a tray with a bowl of soup, a spoon, and crackers.

"You made me feel better with crackers last time. There's ginger ale, too," she says sweetly, and I want to burst into tears all over again.

I take the tray from her. "Thank you, Maggie. This is so sweet of you."

"You did it for me," she says easily. "Try not to eat so much candy this time," she warns, and I laugh.

"I'll make sure to be careful with my candy consumption."

She smiles at me a bit shyly and then runs off toward her room. I take in a deep breath and close the door again, sitting down on the edge of the bed and eating a spoonful of soup.

I suspect she had some help with this from Derek, but the only reason I'm eating it is because Maggie brought it to me.

I don't think that Derek meant any harm by cutting things off with me, but I sure feel rejected and terrible. He doesn't know that was my first time, and now, I'm glad I didn't tell him.

I sigh and finish sipping my soup, eating a few of the crackers just because Maggie found it important to bring them to me. I didn't have much of an appetite, anyway.

I lost my virginity to probably the most attractive man I've ever seen, but at what cost? He doesn't want me, thinks I'm just a little girl. I'm a grown woman, and I wish I could find a way to show him that.

Or maybe... there's a way that I can.

I spend the rest of the week taking care of the kids and then slipping into my room in the evenings, trying to get my courage up, and get a few thin hours of sleep. I set my alarm for five because I know that Derek likes to go into work early, and I put on some natural makeup and curl the ends of my dirty blonde hair. It has gotten a bit longer, a little past my shoulders, and even I have to admit it looks good.

I slide on a pair of denim shorts that I know show off my legs but aren't too revealing, and a low-cut tank top. It looks casual, but sexy. I pout at the mirror, looking at my makeup, and for once, it doesn't feel like I'm a kid playing dress up.

I look good. Pretty, even. I've always thought of myself as plain, but I clean up pretty nice. I take in a deep breath and start downstairs.

I'm right on the money because Derek is in the living

room, putting on his suit jacket and grabbing his watch and keys from the table near the door.

He looks up as I descend the stairs and I swear I can see him do a double take.

"Kenna?"

I look at him. "Mm?"

"You look...you look great," he stutters.

I smile. "Thanks. I have plans with a friend tonight."

Derek's face goes instantly blank. "A friend?"

I nod. "Mmhm," I murmur, as if it's no big deal, and walk into the kitchen to start making the kids some of the Mickey Mouse pancakes they've been obsessed with all week.

Derek usually would be walking out the door by now, but instead, he follows me into the kitchen.

"What kind of friend?"

"Old friend from college," I say easily, bending down to take a pan out of the cabinet. I reach up to grab a mixing bowl but can't quite reach, my shirt riding up to expose part of my belly.

Derek clears his throat, a nervous habit I've noticed of his, and reaches up to grab it for me, his arm brushing against me as he hands it to me.

"Thank you," I mutter, looking up into his eyes, and Derek stares at my mouth for a long moment.

"A friend," he repeats.

I frown. "Why? Did you need me to watch the kids tonight?"

Derek slowly shakes his head. "No. No, I'll be home at six," he says under his breath, as if talking to himself.

I smile. "Okay, then. I'll tell my friend I'll be ready at six."

"They're picking you up? Like a...like a date?" he asks,

and I can feel his eyes on me as I begin to mix up the pancakes.

My friend's name is Cherie and she's my best friend from high school, but Derek doesn't have to know that.

"I guess you could say that," I chirp, and then look at him over my shoulder. "Are you staying for breakfast?"

"No. Better not," he says. "Have...have a good day," he says awkwardly, and then strides back out into the living room and out the door.

I blink, surprised that had worked like I wanted it to. The only thing I know about men I've learned from either my mother or my best friend Cherie. Cherie always says that even if a man doesn't want you, he damn sure doesn't want anyone else to have you. I know this is childish and I shouldn't be misleading him like this, but how else am I supposed to make him realize he wants me. How else am I supposed to know if he actually does?

I sigh.

I hate resorting to such underhanded techniques, but I have to do *something.*

11

———

DEREK

*K*enna's *going on a date tonight.*

The words repeat themselves in my head as I try to work. I'm not getting anything done, and I have a meeting with clients at four. Part of me hopes that I get caught up and don't make it home by six, so that Kenna won't be able to go on her date, but that isn't fair.

Is it?

Just because we hooked up one time doesn't mean I *own* her. But all I can think about today is her smile, her bright blue eyes. She looks like a little Barbie doll sometimes, especially in that getup she was wearing this morning, all long legs and cleavage...

I shift in my office chair, uncomfortable. I have way too much to do today to be worried about Kenna Lodge, but that's what I'm thinking about.

I've been a total bear at the office all morning, barking orders and snapping at people, especially my secretary when she messed up my lunch order. I should apologize.

I feel like I've been doing a lot of that lately, apologizing. Is that why Kenna is going on this date? Is she angry that I

65

apologized? Surely, she didn't take that as some kind of rejection.

Because it isn't a rejection. But does it sound that way? I took advantage of her kind nature and her naïve personality. I'm the bad guy here, but not for the reasons she's thinking.

I wonder if I should explain myself to her when my secretary, Shyla, pops her head in my door.

"Boss?" she asks hesitantly.

I favor her with a big smile, knowing that I've been an ass all morning. "Come in, Shyla. Sit down."

She looks at me warily, her brown eyes wide and untrusting, but she slowly walks inside and sits down across from me at the table.

"Two things," she starts, and then I hold up a hand to stop her.

"First, I want to apologize. I know I've been a jerk today. I just... have a lot on my mind."

Shyla nods, finally smiling a bit. "It's okay, Mr. Ledderman. Don't even think about it."

I sigh in relief. "I'm glad you're so forgiving."

She grins. "If you pay for my lunch, I'll be even more forgiving."

"Consider it done," I say, looking at my watch. "You can take your break now, use my credit card, the one you have on file. Order whatever you like."

"Thank you, Mr. Ledderman." Her shoulders have relaxed, and it seems as if she really has forgiven me. "Just two things before I go. You have your meeting at four with Bradshaw Hospitality."

I inwardly groan but don't say anything. Meeting with Logan Bradshaw's father about doing a marketing campaign for his hotel and hospitality business isn't high up on my list of favorite things to do, but it's a big account and Logan probably doesn't know anything about it. He's gone into the family business but he works in an office out of state, after all. He'd gotten off the West Coast as soon as he could.

"Yes, I remember," I answer.

"And someone's been calling the office, leaving messages for you to call back? They won't leave a name, so I haven't patched them through."

I frown. "Oh yeah?"

She slides a message slip across the desk with just a phone number on it. It isn't an area code I recognize, so I have no idea who it could be.

"Thank you, Shyla. I'll see you in an hour."

Shyla gets up and heads out the door, her heels clicking on the marble floor.

I look at the number for a long moment before getting up to close my door and calling it.

"Hello?"

There's something oddly familiar about the female voice on the other end of the line, but I can't quite place it.

"This is Derek Ledderman. You left a message with my secretary?"

"Several messages," the woman drawls. "Don't you recognize my voice, Derek?"

I frown. "No."

She sighs. "I guess it's been a while. It's Suzie."

I nearly drop my phone but manage to recover, walking back over to my desk and then pacing around the room.

"What the hell do you want?" I snarl.

"Don't worry, your alimony checks have cashed just fine," she says idly. "And you won't have to pay them much longer. I'm getting married in about a month."

"Congratulations," I say flatly, hoping she knows I don't mean it.

"I called because I wanted to give you an opportunity to bring the kids to my wedding."

"When hell freezes over," I growl.

"They're *my* kids, Derek. I gave birth to them."

"That doesn't mean you deserve to be in their life. Eli doesn't even remember what you look like."

Suzanna is quiet for a moment, and I hope she's hung up. This isn't the first time she's called me, asking to see the kids. I even let her see Maggie and Eli a couple of times when they were much younger, but it was never consistent.

"I know I haven't been there for them like I should. I think it's time that I start stepping up to be their mom."

"That ship has sailed, Suzanna. You abandoned them."

"You mean I abandoned *you*," she accuses.

I grit my teeth, trying not to raise my voice. "You abandoned all of us," I say tightly. "But you leaving them is what matters. They don't want to see you. I won't let you see them. Drop it."

"I'll give you a few days to change your mind. I know things are... rocky between us. Maybe you're upset I'm getting married."

I don't give a rat's ass what she was doing, all I can do is feel sorry for the sad sack she roped into marriage.

"But you'll come around," she says easily, and before I can start to yell into the phone, she hangs up.

I curse loudly and I'm glad I have my office doors closed. Today is going to be a hell of a day, and in the back of my mind, still, there's that voice: *Kenna's going on a date tonight.*

I can't catch a fucking break today.

I plaster on a fake smile for the clients, take them to dinner, wine and dine them, although I make sure to keep the same drink the entire time. I'm not in the state of mind to be drinking tonight, given my conversation with Suzanna.

Back at home, I've finally nearly forgotten that Kenna has plans tonight until I see her at the door with her purse.

Fuck.

I told her six, and it's past seven. I really didn't intend to ruin her plans, it's just that with the day I had, everything seemed to go slower than normal.

"Sorry," I mutter as I walk into the house, but Kenna doesn't glare at me, just smiles.

"No problem. My friend's picking me up in a few minutes."

I glance toward the driveway, wondering if I can catch a glance of this guy when he pulls up. Do I even want to?

Do I want to see the guy who might have his hands all over Kenna later? I don't think so.

It's probably better if I just go on inside and spend time with my kids.

"Have a good night," I tell her at the door, watching her smile fade just slightly as I walk inside. Maggie and Eli are putting together a puzzle on the floor, something I could never get them interested in before.

I sit down on the floor with them and focus on the puzzle pieces, my jaw twitching only a little when I hear a car pull up and then drive away.

Kenna's going on a date tonight, I think once more, and then push it out of my mind.

"How many pieces do we have left, kiddos?"

KENNA

I'm lost in my own thoughts when my friend snaps, finally pulling me out of my own head.

"Kenna, it's not like I'm an attention whore or anything, but you've been kind of ignoring me since I picked you up."

I sigh and bang my forehead lightly on the table. We're at a booth at a chain restaurant where we go to get happy hour drinks and appetizers.

Cherie giggles. "You're going through it."

"Shut up," I mumble. "But yeah, I am."

"What's going on? You've got this cushy job now...that place is a *mansion*, Kenna. How did you get it?"

"I met the dad at a coffee shop," I tell her, lifting my head. "And he's like...stupid gorgeous."

Cherie's brown eyes light up. "Oh yeah? Do tell."

He's big and wide and has these green eyes..." I groan. "And...and he kissed me."

"He *what*?" Cherie squeals, and I can't help but laugh at her expression.

I lean across the table, sipping more of my happy hour

margarita for liquid courage. "Not only that. I, um, I lost my virginity."

"To the *dad*?" Cherie screeches, and I reach across the table to cover her mouth with my hand.

"Tell the whole restaurant, why don't you?"

"I'm sorry, Kenna. I'm just *surprised*," she insists. "Not to be a bitch but you were always kind of...well, a prude."

"You *bitch*," I breathe, but then I laugh. I don't mean it. Cherie and I have been friends since high school, so I know I can tell her anything.

Cherie laughs along with me. "I know! I'm sorry. So, you slept with the dad of the kids you're nannying for. You *live* there. Are you gonna hook up with him again?"

"Here's the thing," I say gloomily. "He doesn't want me. He said it was a mistake, apologized, even tried to pay me off."

Cherie gasped. "You're not a hooker."

"That's what I said!" I exclaim. "I don't think he means anything by it, he's just really a good father, Cher, you have no idea. He's a really good guy and I just wish he liked me."

I pout a little, and Cherie reaches across the table to take my hands.

"Any guy would be lucky to hook up with you, Kenna. Maybe you're just one of those people, you know?"

"What people?"

"You know, one of those girls where your heart lies in your..." she gestures down.

I laugh, covering my face for a moment and peeking at her through my fingers. "You mean, someone who gets attached easily once things get physical?"

"Yeah, exactly."

I feel even more gloomy after hearing that. "Yeah, I think

I am," I admit. "And I really like him, but now I feel rejected."

"So, what did you do about it? What did you say?"

I shrug. "Nothing. I need the job, and I love those kids already. He needs my help." I pause. "But I did kind of imply that you were a guy taking me out on a date."

"Good girl," Cherie says with a grin, ordering us another round of margaritas.

"I'm going to have to stay with you tonight if you keep buying me those," I hiccup.

"Absolutely not. You're going to go back to his place tipsy. That way, he'll think you had a great time with your boytoy," Cherie suggests.

"You think so?" I ask her, already on my way to tipsy. I don't drink much, usually.

"Definitely. You have to learn to play the game, Kenna."

"But isn't this a childish game? Shouldn't I want him to see how mature I am?"

"Sure, on both accounts. But you also need him to see you are not a safe thing that will just sit around and wait for him to make up his mind."

To my tipsy brain, her logic makes sense, so I just relax and enjoy the rest of our time together.

When time comes to go home, neither of us is okay to drive. We ate throughout the night, so when we're done, we are not completely wasted, as I thought we would be. I don't even feel as unsteady on my feet.

Instead of calling a cab, though, Cherie calls her boyfriend, Nolan, to take us both home. His eyes nearly bulge out of his head as he pulls up to the gate of Derek's mansion.

When the intercom buzzes and Derek asks who it is in a

hoarse voice, I know he's been asleep and I wince, leaning forward to speak into it.

Cherie kicks the back of my seat. "Let Nolan do it," she hisses.

I blink, not understanding at first, and then giggling to myself as I understand. She wants Derek to think I really did go out with a guy, even though it was just Cherie.

I've got enough alcohol in me to do it, so I let Nolan speak.

He clears his throat. "Uh, dropping off Kenna?"

Derek goes deadly silent and then the gates open wide.

Cherie laughs almost maniacally in the backseat as we pull up to the driveway. Derek doesn't come outside, and I wave goodbye at Cherie and Nolan as I stumble up the stairs. I manage to right myself before letting myself in with the key, and then nearly have a heart attack.

Derek's sitting in the living room in the dark.

"You're late," he says flatly, and I roll my eyes, anger rising in me.

"You're not my dad," I mutter.

He sighs, running a hand through his precociously graying blond hair. "I'm sorry," he mumbles. He stands up and starts to go up the stairs and I follow, albeit slowly so I don't stumble.

When he looks back over his shoulder to see me struggling up the stairs, he grunts in the back of his throat and comes back down, lifting me up over his shoulder like I'm a sack of potatoes.

I just hang there, my head spinning.

"What are you doing?"

"I'm taking you to bed. You can barely walk," he mutters, and he takes me to my room, depositing me not so gently on the bed and looking down at me as I pull the covers around me.

"Did you have fun?" he asks softly.

"So, what if I did?" I shoot back, feeling a little belligerent. After all, he is the one who rejected me.

Derek's brow has been furrowed, a frown on his face, but now his expression goes blank. "Have a good night, Kenna," he says, and walks out of my door, closing it behind him.

Suddenly, tears spring to the backs of my eyes and I don't know if it's the booze or just the rejection that I feel.

It was a stupid plan. *I'm* stupid, and childish, and he's right not to want me.

The next morning is a weekday, so when I wake up at nine in the morning, I wake up in a panic. I'm looking everywhere for my phone but I must have left it in the backseat of Nolan's car.

"Shit, shit, shit," I curse, running downstairs to check on the kids.

Derek is sitting shirtless at the table with a cup of coffee. "Wh-what?"

I'm surprised to see him there, it's so late.

"Taking a day off work," he says gruffly, not looking at me. "I thought you might like a day to recover."

"I don't need a day to recover. I just lost my phone and I didn't have an alarm – you could have woken me up!" I complain.

Derek shrugs. "It's fine. I haven't had a day off since you started working here, anyway. I miss the kids."

I sigh and pour myself a cup of coffee from the pot, sitting down across from him. It occurs to me that I must look like a mess, with my hair all rumpled from sleep, having not even washed my face.

"Do you want me to leave? Go see my parents or something?"

Derek looks up at me for the first time that morning, and I notice the bags under his eyes. He looks like he hasn't slept.

"The kids love it when you're here. Stay," he says, and then looks back down into his coffee.

"Derek?" I ask softly. "Is something...wrong?"

"Suzanna called," he says bluntly, and my eyes widen.

"My aunt Suzanna?"

"The very same. She wants the kids to come to her wedding." He barks out a bitter laugh. "Imagine that."

"That's unacceptable," I say after a long pause. "You're not going to let her see them, are you?"

"Of course not." Derek looks at me curiously. "Although I thought you might try to talk me into it."

I shake my head. "I told you; I don't even know her anymore. My family cut ties with her when she left."

"Still, she's your family."

"Not anymore," I say firmly, finishing my coffee and getting up.

"What are you doing?"

"The kids like my Mickey Mouse pancakes," I say simply.

"You don't have to do that. You're hungover. Let me cook," Derek says, standing up and placing his hand on the small of my back to move me from the refrigerator.

"If you're sure," I say, and plop back down at the kitchen table, my head pounding.

Derek hands me a bottle of water from the fridge, and as I sip it, I watch him move around the kitchen,. After about half the bottle is gone, my headache is much better.

"I probably smell like tequila. I should shower before the kids get up," I say.

"They're already up. I have them watching Paw Patrol in Maggie's room," Derek says.

I laugh. "Whatever works."

"I need at least two cups of coffee before I can handle my little gremlins," he chuckles, mixing something in a big bowl.

I start to walk toward the living room.

"Kenna?"

When I turn to look at him, Derek is staring at me, his green eyes intense.

"Yeah?"

"About last night," he starts, and then trails off.

I stand there, looking at him, swallowing hard. "Yeah?" I repeat dumbly.

"I hope you had a good time," he says quietly, and I kind of want to scream, but instead, I just nod and make my way up the huge staircase.

13

DEREK

I'm dying to know everything about Kenna's night out, including who the guy was who spoke into my intercom at two in the damn morning, but I knew when I gave her this job that she would have her own life.

She's my nanny, not my girlfriend.

So, why does it make me seethe just thinking about someone else's hands on her?

And now I have Suzanna trying to wiggle her way back into our lives.

I roll my shoulders around, trying to stop feeling tense as I finish up breakfast.

"Mickey Mouse pancakes?" Eli asks, rubbing his eyes as he comes down the stairs. Dollars to donuts he went back to sleep after climbing in bed with Maggie to watch television this morning. Maggie is a morning person. Eli, not so much.

"Dad's famous biscuits and gravy," I say, preparing myself for a tantrum.

Instead, Eli's little arms go around me and he hugs my legs from behind. "I like it when you're home to make breakfast, Daddy," he says softly, and I turn around to tickle him and pick him up. He squeals in glee and then Maggie stomps down the stairs.

"Where's Kenna?" Maggie demands to know, and I laugh and put Eli into his booster seat in one of the dining room chairs.

"She's taking a shower, Magpie. She'll be down in a minute."

Her hazel eyes light up. "So, we're having breakfast with Kenna *and* Daddy?"

I smile. "If that's okay."

Maggie giggles and sits next to Eli, grabbing her fork as if she's ready to eat right now.

The kids are so attached to Kenna already. I'd almost messed all of that up, and for what? A one-night stand with a woman nearly half my age?

I make each of the kids a plate and one for me and Kenna, too, and she comes down freshly showered and smelling like rosewater, her dirty blonde hair damp.

"It smells amazing, Derek," she says as I sit at the end of the table.

The kids eat plenty and Kenna asks for seconds, and overall, we have a wonderful breakfast. Eli tells me all about how Kenna told him a story about trains that run on magic and Maggie corrects him twice and tells him they run on *unicorn* magic.

She's wonderful with them. She talks with them and laughs with them and I would never have found a better nanny.

I just have to keep it together, and push down my jealousy about her new boyfriend. Even the thought of it makes me want to grit my teeth, so I try not to think about it.

I'm a simple man.

If it hurts, I won't think about it. It's easy.

But not thinking about it is kind of like not thinking about the elephant in the room, and when Maggie and Eli both pass out in a few hours after finishing the floor puzzle with Kenna, we find ourselves alone again.

I don't quite know what to do with myself in social situations that aren't work related.

"Do you want to keep receiving cash? Or I could talk to my accountant about direct deposit?" I mumble, and Kenna looks at me, confused.

"Oh, cash is fine," she says back, blushing slightly. "You pay me too much, though."

"I don't pay you enough," I shoot back.

Maggie snorts out a snore and Eli whines when she kicks him in the head.

"I should take them up to bed," I say, laughing softly.

"I'll take Eli, you take Maggie," she says, and I nod.

I pick up my little girl and she tucks her head against my shoulder immediately. I'm filled suddenly with love for her and Eli, thinking that I never would have made it through Suzanna leaving if they weren't with me.

I wish she was a better mother to them, but at the same time, I'm so glad they're mine and mine alone that I can barely stand it.

They're perfect, despite all their attitude problems now and again.

Kenna takes Eli up to his room and I take Maggie to hers, lying her down gently and kissing her forehead. She snores even louder on her back and I can't help smiling as I tuck her in.

I meet Kenna in the hallway, and again, I don't know what to say.

"Derek," she says before I slip into my room just to get out of the situation.

"Yes?"

"Last night," she starts.

I hold up a hand, planning to tell her it's none of my business, that I'm sorry I pried, but she shakes her head, continuing.

"It's not what you think," is all she says, and then she disappears into her room.

I take in a deep breath. Living with Kenna after kissing her, touching her, being with her, is going to be a real challenge.

I stand out in the hallway for a long moment before I curse under my breath and knock lightly on her door.

"Come in," she calls, and she's standing in front of the bed, biting her lip.

"The guy you saw last night," I start, not sure where I'm even going with this. "Is he going to be around a lot?"

"Why do you ask?"

Her face is blank. I can't read her, not like I read the clients that I'm talking into parting with hundreds of thousands of dollars for marketing campaigns.

I can't tell her the real reason that I'm asking. I can't tell her that it's driving me crazy, every moment I think about what might have happened, every moment I imagine someone else's hands on her.

"Just curious," I mumble. "I just like to know the type of people that might be hanging around here."

"No other reason?" she asks, taking another step toward me.

Fuck, she smells so good. She's so pretty, looking at me with those wide, almost innocent eyes. I'm such a dirty old man.

"What other reason would there be?"

Kenna bites her lip and I want to groan, want to pull her

into my arms and pop that pouty bottom lip from between her teeth.

"I won't bring him around the kids," is all she says, and I want to pull my hair out.

"So, you'll be meeting him somewhere else?"

Kenna stiffens her shoulders. "I'm allowed to meet whoever I want on my own time."

"Of course you are," I mutter, running a hand through my hair.

Jealousy is such a horrible emotion. I've always hated it, and I've never had much reason to feel that way since Suzanna left, so it feels doubly awful.

"Sorry," I say, stepping backward out into the hall.

"If you don't want me to see anyone else, just say so," Kenna says firmly, something flashing in her blue eyes.

"I can't ask that of you."

Kenna takes another step forward, and now I'm standing in her doorway, half in the hallway and half in her room.

"You can," she says softly, and then she wraps her arms around my neck.

"Kenna," I breathe, and I don't know how that sentence would have ended, don't know if I would have kissed her, given it all up just for another taste of her, because the doorbell rings.

It startles me because I've been so lost in Kenna, and I clear my throat. Her face falls just as her arms do.

"Excuse me."

I make my way downstairs, peering into the cameras and I have no idea how this person got through the gate so I'm suspicious, looking out the peephole.

It's just a man in a suit, and I wonder if a solicitor has gotten ahold of the gate code again. I haven't changed it since we moved here, so maybe it's time.

I open the door.

"Derek Ledderman?" the man looks up at me, much shorter than me and balding.

"Yes?"

He hands me a manilla envelope. "You've been served."

14

KENNA

I follow Derek down the stairs hesitantly. It's really none of my business who's at the door, but I'm curious, especially since whoever it is interrupted what could have been an important moment for me.

It's not like I expected Derek to confess, to tell me that he's fallen in love with me, or anything like that. But if I'm honest with myself, I secretly *did* hope that's what he was planning on doing.

I frown when Derek slams the door shut, cursing.

He's flipping through paperwork when I get down to the living room.

"Is everything okay? What's that?" I ask, curious.

"It's fine," he mutters, stalking past me and up the stairs again.

"Derek," I start, but then he cuts me off.

"It's none of your business, Ms. Lodge," he barks, walking into his office upstairs and shutting the door.

Ms. Lodge? So, we're back to that, are we?

Tears sting at the backs of my eyes and I fight them back, biting my lip. There's no reason that I even need to be here, since Derek is home and can take care of the kids. I should have never stayed when he took the day off.

This is stupid. I don't belong here. This is just my job. He's just my boss. He's made that abundantly clear.

I gather my things quietly and leave the house, heading toward my parents' house.

I make it just a couple of blocks before I start to cry.

When I walk into my parents' house, my father is nowhere to be found and my brother meets me at the door, his brow furrowed.

"Something's wrong with Dad," he says.

"Wh-what?" I blink, my eyes still feeling raw from crying all the way home.

"He's locked himself in his office and Mom won't talk to us," Ryan remarks. "You've got to fix it, Kenna."

He looks at me with something pleading in his blue eyes, so much like mine, and I take in a deep breath. It doesn't matter what's going on with me and my job. I need to be here for my family, too, and suddenly, I feel like I've been neglecting that part of my life.

I pull my much larger brother into a hug and he's stiff the whole time but he hugs me back.

"Sorry I haven't been home," I say softly, and he pulls away from me.

"Don't you start being weird too," he teases, and I smile.

My brother isn't the best with words or with asking for help, but I can always read between the lines.

When I get to my father's office, the door is locked and I can hear hushed voices.

"She's my sister," my father says mournfully. "How do I do this?"

"It's not your fault that she made those decisions," my mother says.

I frown, knocking on the door lightly.

There's a shuffling sound from behind the door and my mother opens it, finally, and gives a sigh of relief when she sees me. "Kenna. I'm so glad you're here."

"What's going on?" I ask.

My father is sitting behind his desk with his head in his hands. "Your aunt Suzanna, that's what," he barks.

"Don't snap at her," my mother scolds. "It's not her fault."

"Sorry, Ken," Dad mutters, and Mom hugs me, patting my back before pulling away.

"Your aunt called your father. She wants him to testify in court."

I blink. "What? Is she in trouble again?"

Dad shakes his head. "No more than usual."

"She wants to get custody of the kids," Mom explains, sounding exasperated.

"She can't do that!" I exclaim, and Dad looks up at me.

"She's their mother. There's a possibility she can," he says.

"You see the position this puts your father in."

"Not really," I say stubbornly. "She's not a good mother. That's all he has to say."

"She's my baby sister, Kenna. It's not that simple," my father argues.

I think about it. If Ryan or Kimberly abandoned their family the way that Suzanna abandoned theirs, could I go in court and testify that they were bad parents? I don't know for sure, and I can start to understand why my father is so upset.

"I'm sorry, Dad. This puts you between a rock and a hard place." I sit down across from him.

"You know that she'll ask you to testify, too, now that you're nannying for Derek," my father points out.

Shit.

I hadn't thought of that. "I haven't heard anything," I say hopefully.

"We just heard today. We went back and forth for a while, but she says she needs all the help she can get."

"You're not going to testify, are you?" I ask, and my father looks up at me for a long moment.

"No. No, I don't think I will. I love my sister, but I can't lie in court or defend her actions. It's just a difficult spot to be in."

"What about you, Kenna?" Mom asks. "Are you going to testify?"

"Not for Suzanna," I say firmly.

"Since you're one of their caretakers, you'll have to testify," my father explains.

I bite my lip. It *is* a weird position to be in for my father, but for me? I barely know Aunt Suzanna. Hell, even after the time I spent working for him, I don't know that much about Derek.

But I know those kids. I know Maggie and Eli, and I know that they love their father. I know that he's there for them, every single day. And Suzanna hasn't seen them in years.

"I'll testify, but not for her." I say again. "I'll testify for Derek."

Mom looks a bit shocked, but my father nods.

"He's always been a good dad," he agrees.

I think back to earlier. No wonder Derek snapped at me. He must be going through so much. I feel guilty for thinking poorly of him, but at the same time, he *has* made it clear that he's not interested in me. It's time to let it go.

He needs to focus on his family, and I need to focus on mine.

"I just want what's best for the kids," I say, and that's true. It doesn't matter what's best for me or Derek or Suzanna. It matters what's best for Maggie and Eli. "Who do I need to talk to in order to testify?"

"Derek," my mother says. "Or his lawyer."

I nod slowly. I don't know if I want to go through Derek, because I don't want him thinking that I'm overstepping my bounds.

But I have no idea who Derek's lawyer is. There are a lot of expensive family lawyers in Los Angeles, and it could be any of them.

I might have to talk to Derek, after all, and admit I know what's going on.

I spend the night at my parents' house, trying to decide how to get in contact with Derek's lawyer, but it ends up not mattering, because the next morning, I get a phone call.

"Hello, is this McKenna Lodge?"

"Yes," I answer quickly, sitting up in bed. I'd been awake, just staring at the ceiling.

"Brett Reynolds," the man says. "I'm Derek Ledderman's lawyer. I was wondering if you'd have some time today to come into my office and speak about his upcoming custody case?"

I'm surprised that he called me so quickly, since it's only been a day since Derek was served. I guess expensive lawyers are expensive because they're good, at least in this case.

"I can be there in half an hour," I say, and half an hour later, I find myself at the offices of Reynolds and Platt.

It's a *nice* office, with a chandelier in the lobby, and I only have to wait a few moments but I'm offered cucumber water while I sit there. I accept a glass and then Brett Reynolds calls me into his office.

"Thank you for agreeing to come on such short notice, Ms. Lodge," he greets me, gesturing for me to sit down in the chair across from his desk.

I do so and the lawyer looks at me discerningly.

"You've been working as a nanny for Derek Ledderman for the last couple of months?" he asks.

"Not quite two months," I answer.

He nods. "But you spend a lot of time with Margaret and Eli Ledderman, right?"

"I do. I'm with them every weekday, and Derek has them in the evenings and the weekends."

"Would you say that you stay with them more than their father does?"

I frown. "I don't like that question."

Brett gives me an apologetic smile. "Sorry. I guess I'm getting ahead of myself. You see, I'm going to ask you to testify in court as one of the kids' caretakers. The other lawyer is going to ask you things like that."

"The answer is that I don't spend any more time with them than say, a daycare worker would. Derek comes home on time every single night and he does things with them every weekend. He spends every moment he's not at work with those kids."

"Perfect. I think you'll do wonders for Mr. Ledderman's case, Ms. Lodge."

I smile hesitantly. "That's good to hear. Will Derek know that I'm testifying?"

"He has character witnesses that he's choosing, but in terms of your testimony, you'll be interviewed by me and Ms. Lodge's lawyer because you're considered one of their caretakers," he explains. "Your testimony is completely up to you. I understand Suzanna Lodge is your aunt?"

"Estranged," I say tightly.

Brett makes a note. "I think you'll help out his case, but it depends on what you say in court, Ms. Lodge. Do you understand?"

I nod slowly. "I think so."

"The custody hearing is scheduled on the twenty-fifth, a week from today. I was able to get it expedited. I don't want Mr. Ledderman to have to deal with this any longer than he has to. If you'll meet with me the day before the hearing, we'll go over your testimony one last time."

"Sounds good." I stand up and go to leave.

"Ms. Lodge?"

I turn. "Yes?"

"You shouldn't talk to anyone about the case, of course, not until it's over."

Of course I wouldn't. Especially not to Derek. I don't want to stress him out any more than he already is.

15

DEREK

For all of Suzanna's yearly phone calls to check on the kids and even the call she'd made to my office, I never thought that it would come to this.

She served me *papers*. She thinks that she can wiggle her way back into my kids' lives after being gone since they were babies, and it infuriates me.

I shouldn't have snapped at Kenna, but the fact that she's related to Suzanna makes me wary sometimes. She's wonderful with the kids and they love her, but she's just unlucky enough to be related to one of the worst people in the world.

It doesn't fill me with confidence that she'll testify for me in court. In fact, I think she might side with her aunt.

She says they're estranged, but doesn't everyone want their family to be okay and have what they want? I'm not exactly close to my aunts and uncles, and I haven't talked to any of them in years, but would I testify for them as character witnesses? Probably.

Of course, none of them had done what Suzanna did.

None of them abandoned their husband and two children without so much as a word.

It would have been different, maybe, if Suzanna had *talked* to me. If she had told me she was feeling overwhelmed, let me help her...

But she didn't. And it isn't like she started reaching out to see the kids right away. It had taken over a year for her even to call and check on them.

It's clear to me that she views our kids as some kind of pets that she can put away in a kennel when she doesn't want to deal with them.

I hope Brett Reynolds can help me prove that in court.

When Kenna comes to the mansion on Monday morning, I meet her at the door, standing in the doorjamb.

"Take the week off," I say bluntly, and Kenna just stares at me.

"The whole week?"

"Taking some vacation time," I explain, trying to keep things light. I don't want her having any reason to dislike me and testify against me.

And god, what if she mentions that we slept together? That would make me look like a terrible father, sleeping with the nanny.

I want to ask her to not bring it up, but I don't know how. In the end, that's the lawyer's job.

"Are you sure you don't need help around the house?" Kenna asks, biting her full bottom lip.

I glance down at her mouth before looking back into her blue eyes. "It's all right. I want to spend time with the kids."

"Tell them I said hello," Kenna says hesitantly before going back to her car.

I shut the door and Maggie stares up at me. She apparently heard the whole conversation.

"What is it, Magpie?"

"Why don't you want Kenna to play with us all week?" she demands to know.

"Because I want to spend my vacation with you kiddos, not our nanny."

"Daddy," Maggie says matter-of-factly. "She's more than our nanny. She's our friend."

I force a smile and try to get her distracted by television or puzzles, but she's stuck on the subject and asks me again.

"Kenna's still your friend when she's not here," I say finally, exasperated. "She said to tell you hello."

"Can I call her?" Maggie asks, and I take in a deep breath.

"Maybe later."

Eli and Maggie finally begin playing with the Easy Bake Oven and I can finally relax and try not to think about everything going on.

It occurs to me that this week might be the perfect time for Kenna's new boyfriend to sweep her off her feet, but I can't think about that right now. My jealousy and my feelings for my children's nanny are secondary to keeping my family together. No matter how she testifies, I need to make sure that we're okay.

I call Loxton first.

"Listen, do you think that you could be a character witness for me?" I ask.

"A character witness? What'd you do?" Loxton asks immediately, and I chuckle bitterly, low in the back of my throat.

"Married Suzanna Lodge," I mutter. "She's trying to take the kids."

"Bullshit," Loxton curses. "We won't let that happen."

I call Grayson next. He says yes immediately, too, inviting me to come and talk to him anytime.

"You know that I know what it's like to have your kid taken from you," he reminds me.

I sigh in relief. I knew they would testify, and I'm trying to get ahold of Logan, too, since they've all known me for longer than anyone that I work with. They're really the only friend group I've ever had, and I really need them right now.

I spend the rest of the day giving out Brett Reynolds number to friends and colleagues and even a couple of daycare workers who have watched Maggie and Eli on a drop-in basis.

All I can do is pray that everything goes well.

The second day, I feel stir crazy, so I take the kids with me to Grayson's. Maggie and Grayson's son get along well, and Eli loves to hold the baby girl, so they'll be distracted while we talk.

Maggie and Max run off to play with Max's toys and Eli plops down, waiting to hold the baby. Lilian brings her over and puts her in his arms.

I manage to snap a couple of pictures before I go into Grayson's office, leaving Lilian to keep an eye on the kids.

"She's trying to take full custody?" Grayson asks.

"Can you believe it?"

He snorted. "Unfortunately, I can. Your alimony is about to dry up, right? And she seems to need to maintain a certain lifestyle. She seems like the type that wants everything a certain way, and if she needs to use the kids like that, too bad."

"You're right. I know you are. I just hope that the judge sees it that way too."

"Derek, don't worry. Reynolds is a shark. He was willing

to track Lilian down and serve her with papers for me, but I never went through with it."

"Lucky you," I mutter.

Grayson smiles evenly. "Lucky me, it all worked out in the end. It will for you, too." He pauses, looking at me. "What about your nanny situation? Do you think she'll tell the whole truth?"

I wince. "I think that'd be pretty damaging to my case, so I hope not. I hope she keeps our personal life private."

Grayson raises a groomed eyebrow. "Your personal life? Are you still sleeping with her?"

"God, no," I say, although I've certainly been thinking about it. I guess you could say, given my fantasies when I'm alone, that I'm sleeping with her in my head.

"I'm glad you figured it out and she didn't quit. I know how much you need the help."

"Do you think it'll look bad that I have a nanny at all? Should I fire her?" I ask, suddenly worried.

"Don't make any rash decisions right now," Grayson warns. "That looks bad for stability. The kids have been in your house, in your care, since they were born. You have sufficient childcare for your work schedule. That's all that matters."

I know from hearing about other cases where the mother got custody that isn't always the case, but I don't argue, just gloomily sipping the coffee Lilian made me.

"It'll all be over soon," Grayson says, clapping me on the back.

Eli doesn't want to leave and starts yelling, and then Maggie starts crying for Kenna, and I'm about to pull my hair out when we arrive back at the house.

I already miss Kenna, and not just how pretty she is and how good she smells. She's good at her job, and maybe I was wrong to give her the week off just because I'm worried about what she might say in court.

I think about calling her and asking her to come back, but in the end, I don't, just nursing a glass of whiskey and looking down at my phone.

I don't know how to feel about Kenna anymore, if I ever did.

16

KENNA

The week without work goes by painfully slowly. I spend a lot of time with my brother and sister and my parents, though. We're all trying to get Dad's mind off the upcoming court case. He feels bad for not testifying for Derek, and bad for not testifying for Suzanna, and it's just a bad situation for him.

The court date is on Friday, so on Thursday, I make my way to the lawyer's office.

There are several people milling around in the lobby today, including a couple of men in what looks like ten-thousand-dollar suits. They're both handsome, and all I can figure is that they're colleagues of Derek's.

I'm called in after the second man comes out, and Brett asks me a series of rapid fire questions that I stumble over.

"Do you have any contact with Suzanna Lodge?" *No, not for years.*

"How well do you know Derek Ledderman?" *Fairly well, we've been in close quarters for two months now.*

"How many days a week do you take care of Margaret

and Eli Ledderman?" *I work five days a week, Monday through Friday.*

"Do you have an appropriate relationship with your employer?"

I freeze at that last question.

"Why are you asking me that?"

"Because that's what her lawyer is going to ask you," he says simply. "They're going to try and find cracks in the kids' stability anywhere they can."

"I have an appropriate relationship with my employer," I finally answer, and Brett smiles.

"Very good, Ms. Lodge."

It doesn't feel very good, to lie in court, but what else am I supposed to do? Tell the courtroom that Derek and I had slept together? What good would that do other than possibly losing custody of Maggie and Eli?

I can't let that happen.

I barely sleep that night. I'm at the courthouse at nine in the morning, even though the hearing isn't until eleven-thirty, and they call me in at noon.

The woman representing Suzanna is dressed in what looks like a *very* expensive pantsuit and she has a sneer on her face from the moment I enter the room.

I don't hear the first parts of the trial or Derek's character witnesses, just waiting my turn in the lobby. Even testifying, in a way, feels like I'm overstepping.

I'm only a nanny, after all.

"How do you know the plaintiff?" Suzanna's lawyer asks once I'm sworn in.

"She's my paternal aunt," I say woodenly. Suzanna's smiling at me from the pews, but I ignore her.

"And are you close with her?"

"Not particularly, no. I haven't spoken to her in years."

The lawyer hums. "Yet, you currently watch her children, correct?"

"I watch Mr. Ledderman's children," I say flatly, and the lawyer checks her notes.

"Monday through Friday, six in the morning until six at night, is that correct?"

"Yes." She isn't asking anything particularly wild, at least not yet, but I'm wary.

"When does Mr. Ledderman spend time with his children?"

"Every moment that he's not at work," I say confidently. I look over at Derek but he's looking down at his hands.

"And you've seen this?"

"Well, sometimes. I usually go home or make myself scarce so that they have time together, but he's taken mornings and full days off to spend with them. He's wonderful with the kids."

The questioning goes on, but she never asks if I have an appropriate relationship with my employer the way that Brett said she might.

I let out a long breath of relief leaving the courtroom. I don't know how the case will pan out, but I've done my part.

I know that I should go home, wait to hear the results from Derek himself, but instead, I hang around in the parking garage near my car. I want to make sure he's okay, no matter how it went.

I see him coming around the corner, loosening his tie with a thunderous expression on his face, and suddenly I'm afraid. What if everything did go wrong? What if he blames me for it? What if I'm fired now?

"Kenna?" Derek frowns, squinting at me in the dark of the parking garage.

I clear my throat and step out from behind one of the

pillars. "I wasn't stalking you; just was curious as to how things went."

"They went great," he admits, breaking into a big smile. "You helped me out so much back there, Kenna, I don't know what to do to repay you."

My shoulders slump in relief. I didn't realize how worried I was about it until I heard it turned out fine.

"You don't have to do anything to repay me," I say simply. "I just told the truth."

"You didn't have to help me," Derek murmurs, walking closer. "Especially after what happened, and I'm so grateful."

I look up at him, slightly nervous that he's so close. Usually, when Derek gets this close, something happens.

"I didn't have to help you, but those kids love you, Derek. You're what's best for them, not my aunt."

"I was worried you'd testify for her."

My face goes blank as I try not to be angry. I can't believe he would think that I'd choose to testify for her after the time I spent working for him, being with him and the kids.

I'm suddenly not feeling very well, the world tilting slightly on its axis, and I start to walk back toward my car.

Derek grabs my wrist, turning me around and pulling me to him.

I gasp, looking up into his eyes but before I can speak, he leans down to kiss me. It isn't hungry or searching like it has been before, but somehow just sweet, like a reward.

It almost feels like goodbye.

He pulls away slowly. "You'll be available to start work again on Monday?" he asks.

"Sure thing, boss," I say, and he grins at me again. He really is so handsome when he smiles.

Derek walks past me up to his car and I get into mine, breathing a bit too hard.

Is that it? Is that my reward?

Just one kiss?

I can't help but be bitterly disappointed. But in the end, I don't want Derek to give me something as a reward. I don't want him to want me because I helped him. I want him to want me because I'm me and because he's in love with me, truth be told.

I'm a mess who's in love with her employer after two scant months.

I feel dizzy again and shake my head, trying to rid myself of the feeling, before driving back to my parents' house.

Monday morning, I punch in the code to the gate, which Derek had told me after the fiasco with me going out with Cherie.

Eli and Maggie come running at me like little crazy people as soon as I open the door, and Eli jumps up into my arms, so suddenly I stumble backward.

"Hey there, kiddos," I hum and Maggie hugs my waist as tightly as she can.

"Don't go away so long next time, Kenna," she says.

Eli's kissing all over my face and I laugh. "I promise; I won't," I say easily.

Derek walks into the living room in his suit but without his jacket, sipping coffee, and I can see his eyes crinkle up with a smile.

It's hard to fight this feeling that I'm right where I belong.

17

DEREK

I keep hoping that Kenna will become less attractive to me somehow, but after she'd testified on my behalf, I'm grateful to her on top of being attracted to her, and it's not getting any easier. I keep looking at her mouth when she comes in the mornings, seeing the curve of her ass when she leaves at night.

It's a week before we get any alone time together, because the kids are all over her all the time after her week away, and simply because I have too much work.

I find myself cranky, irritable, and Kenna raises an eyebrow at me when I curse and slam my hand on the counter when I can't get the coffeemaker to work.

"Did the coffeemaker do something to offend you?" she teases.

"Yeah, it won't fucking work," I mutter.

"You need to learn to relax, Mr. Ledderman."

I sigh. She's been calling me that ever since the court date. She hasn't called me Derek since, and I don't know why it bothers me so much, but it does. I suppose her calling me by my first name feels more intimate, and as much as I try to fight it, I do want to be close with Kenna.

"I've already taken all my vacation days stressing out over the hearing," I point out.

She shrugs. "So, just take a weekend." She points outside. "You have that big pool that you never use, just take the weekend and have nothing but some good music that you like, some cocktails, and relaxation."

I pause. "You know what? That's not such a bad idea." My mother has been on my ass to see the kids, anyway.

"Maybe I'll take the kids for a pool day today," Kenna muses, as if mostly to herself. "I got a new bikini."

I freeze, nearly spilling my coffee. *Please don't be wearing a bikini when I get home*, I think but can't bring myself to say. I've already been an ass about who she sees, I can't also be an ass about what she wears.

Speaking of who she's seeing, Kenna hasn't said word one about the guy she's been spending time with and it's beginning to irk me. My irritation keeps growing and growing and I don't know how to stop it. It's probably also the fact that between the hearing and work, I haven't taken myself in hand, well...in a long time. It's been a long while since I've had some relief, so to speak.

Kenna in a bikini would not solve my problems. In fact, would probably create more of them.

"You don't have plans this week?" I ask her, hiding behind my coffee.

"Not this week," she says breezily, as if it depends on the week.

"Your boyfriend doesn't miss you?" I ask, and Kenna turns from the window to look at me.

She shrugs. "Who knows?"

That's not an answer, and it's making me feel even more

hot under the collar, so I huff out a breath and get up, kissing the kids goodbye before walking out the door.

She'll have a hard time trying to get them in the pool, but I don't tell her that. Let her find out for herself.

When they were smaller, the pool was all they wanted to do, but as they got older it was all about screentime. I haven't been able to get them to play outside for ages.

Maybe I'm being grumpy for no reason, but Kenna has to do trial and error just like I did.

At work, time seems to creep by. I keep watching the clock, waiting for five in the afternoon, even though I can really leave anytime I want to.

Being my own boss, essentially, means I have my own hours. But I know work needs to be done, and I need to stay until at least five.

I get out of the office at four-forty-five, unable to stand it any longer. When I arrive home, the house is empty and I walk out to the back patio, where Maggie is doing a cannonball into the pool with her floaties on and Kenna sits with Eli at the wading end, watching her and laughing.

Eli paddles into the pool when I walk around to the edge of it.

"Daddy, look! Kenna's teaching me to swim!"

"You're doing great, bud," I call to him, and Maggie dog-paddles back to the ladder to jump in all over again, holding her nose.

Kenna stands up to face me and I try my best not to let my eyes scan down her body. The bikini isn't inappropriate or anything, it covers everything important, but the lines of her body are hard to look away from. She's curvy in all the right places but with athletic, long, coltish legs, and I'm beginning to get a headache from purposefully not looking down.

"So, you managed to get them in the pool," I say to Kenna, and she grins.

"What kind of kids don't like the pool?" she asks.

"My kids, usually," I mumble. "You're working wonders with them, Kenna."

"Happy to do it," she says. " They're great kids."

I look at her, standing there in the sunlight in her bikini with water beaded on her body, and my mouth goes dry.

"I'll get out of your hair after a shower," Kenna says, and starts to walk inside. I take hold of her hand to stop her and she turns, surprise evident on her face.

"Why don't you join us for dinner? I'll cook something nice."

She blinks at me. "Well, okay. That's an offer I can't refuse. Your breakfast was so good last time."

I give her a wide smile and tell the kids dinner will be ready in an hour.

I dig out some steaks I had deep in my refrigerator for the last few days, having neglected to cook them. I season them with a crust and grill them outside, making some quick boxed mashed potatoes and some canned vegetables to go with them. Although I can order out every meal I want, I like the idea of my kids having a homecooked meal most nights.

Kenna sniffs in the direction of the grill. Having shed my suit jacket and shirt, I'm now cooking in my slacks and bare feet.

"It smells amazing," she praises.

"It'll taste even better," I promise, and indeed, it does. I have to say so myself that the steak is delectable, and even the boxed mashed potatoes are creamy and good.

The kids pick at the vegetables and eat cut up pieces of steak and mashed potatoes. They seem more well behaved, happier when Kenna is here. She's really good for them, and when, late at night, I can't stop thinking about her blue eyes, I remember that.

I can't mess this up just because I'm attracted to her.

"Are you married, Kenna?" Maggie asks, and I choke on my wine.

"I'm not," Kenna says easily, smiling.

"But you have a boyfriend," Eli pipes up, surprisingly. I wonder if he'd overheard my conversation from this morning.

"Sure I do," Kenna says, just as easily, and I stiffen. "His name is Eli."

Eli blushes a cherry red and hides under the table while Maggie laughs, and the subject is dropped, just like that. Kenna's good with that, too, changing the kids' conversations away from topics that might be hard to talk about, but listening to them, too.

She really is the perfect nanny.

"Have you decided about your relaxing weekend?" Kenna asks me.

I look over at Maggie and Eli. "How do you guys feel about staying with Nana this weekend?"

Eli pops up from the table and his eyes light up. "Will Nana have peas to shell?"

"I don't know why you like shelling peas," Maggie grumbles. "It's boring."

"You like *eating* peas," Eli shoots back, scrunching up his nose.

Kenna smiles. "I like peas, too."

"Gross!" Eli groans, fake gagging and falling over dramatically.

"Okay, okay, I think it's bath time, isn't it?" I stand and sweep Eli up over my shoulder. Maggie follows primly.

I stand outside the door when Maggie showers. She's gotten to the age where she enjoys her privacy, so I just stand there to make sure she doesn't need anything or make the water too hot. The door stays cracked open and she calls to me.

"What's up, Magpie?"

"Why don't you marry Kenna?"

I freeze outside the door, banging my head slightly on the wall behind me. "Because she's our nanny, Maggie."

"There's no laws against marrying nannies," she says matter-of-factly, but luckily for me, she drops it, singing a song and dancing around in the shower. I smile, hearing her shuffle around.

When she comes out, she only has her top on backward, so I remove it and put it on the right way.

"You're getting good at dressing yourself," I praise.

Maggie beams and crawls into bed. She likes her sleep and doesn't fight it, like Eli always does. I spent many nights awake, trying to get him to sleep, even before Suzanna left.

I spent so many nights not sleeping after she left, for more reasons than just helping Eli calm down.

I'm so glad that now I have full custody of the kids, and that Suzanna wasn't able to upend our lives like she wanted, but I know that when Maggie and Eli are older, they'll have questions. They might even want to see her.

I can't stop them, can't protect them from her. Not then, at least. But I can now, and I have. Thanks in part, to Kenna.

It's possible that I still would have won the case without her testimony, but I think it went a long way to convincing the judge that I have a stable life for the kids. Not to mention her praise about me being a good dad. It made my heart swell.

Eli's bath takes longer, and he doesn't want to go to bed, whining.

"Kenna sings me a story," he says, and I chuckle.

"You mean sings you a song?"

"No," he says pointedly, pouting. "She sings me a *story*."

Eli's bedtime is at seven, so Kenna often puts him to bed if I'm working late. I guess he's gotten used to her methods.

"Kenna's busy," I say, but then there's a voice coming from behind me.

"Not too busy," Kenna says, wearing a towel, her blonde hair up in a bun. She's still in her bikini and must have been getting ready to shower. She often checks in on the kids before bed.

"What kind of story this time, Eli? About the conductor?"

Eli nods eagerly, and Kenna perches on the bed next to me, her thigh bumping mine. It's very frustrating how hard my heart starts to hammer away inside my chest at her nearness.

Kenna sings a silly song about a train conductor who comes across a magical land, and I can't help but smile, especially when Eli closes his eyes tight.

"Good job, Eli. Imagine the conductor. Imagine the magical world, with the unicorns—"

"And dragons," Eli all but whispers.

"And the dragons. And you'll have good dreams."

Eli's asleep within moments, and I stare at Kenna, surprised.

"He goes to sleep so easily with you," I marvel as we walk out into the hallway, shutting Eli's door halfway. He likes to keep it open in case he has another nightmare. They'd ramped up during the week I was home, I suppose because he could sense my stress.

"He told me he's afraid of bad dreams," she says. "So, I told him to think about the story we tell at night and he'll have better dreams."

"It works like a charm."

Kenna favors me with a big, toothy smile. "I'm glad it helps him."

"Kenna," I say, and she looks up at me, tilting her head, still smiling. "I really want you to know how much I appreciate you and what you've done for us."

Kenna blushes. "Don't mention it, Mr. Ledderman. You've done a lot for me too. This job has been a dream."

The job.

I find it hard sometimes to think of Kenna as an employee. She fits so well into our little family, and I don't know how to reconcile that with my attraction to her.

"You've been a dream employee," I tell her, and Kenna smiles again, looking away.

"Thank you."

"I also wanted to thank you for not mentioning...what happened between us....at the hearing."

Kenna's smile fades. "Why would I have mentioned that?"

I shrug, panicking a little because it seems like she's a little upset. Before I can speak again, she shakes her head.

"Don't mention it, Mr. Ledderman."

Shit.

I'd gone and put my foot in my mouth again.

18

KENNA

The second I think things are going in the right direction with Derek, he changes course. He was so kind to me, telling me how grateful he was, but then he mentioned the hearing and how I didn't tell them that we had slept together. Why would I have told them that? What kind of person does he think I am?

He really thought that I would have testified for Suzanna and also outed him about us hooking up. I would only have done that if I had no interest in what the kids really needed.

It isn't fair. He has this idea of me as a naïve little girl, or worse, an actively vengeful rejected mate. I guess I'd just keep calling him Mr. Ledderman forever.

DEREK DRIVES the kids to their grandmother's house a couple of hours away, and tells me he might not be home that night. It's a Friday, and I have absolutely nothing better to do, so I make myself some cocktails using Derek's expensive vodka and take it out to the pool on Friday evening. It's nearing dusk and a little cold out, but the pool is heated and when I slip down into the water, I sigh in relief.

I've been feeling oddly achy over the last few days, dizzy on and off, but I think I'm finally getting better. I have good days and bad days, and I guess the stress of this whole situation just got the best of me.

It's nice to relax, especially with no one in the house. I haven't ever lived alone, and I guess this is what it would be like...if I was a billionaire, anyway.

I tilt my head back, looking up at the stars and sipping my drink. It seems to be going to my head quicker than normal, but I guess it doesn't matter. The kids aren't here and Derek won't be home tonight.

I go for a couple of laps and then tread water in the middle of the pool, feeling a little tipsy but none the worse for wear.

I don't hear Derek's car when it pulls up. I see him walk around the corner of the house, though, and I squeak as he walks out to the pool after going into the house.

"You decided to take over my pool, I see," he says, and I don't know if he's angry or not, so I just keep treading water, looking up at him.

"Sorry," I chirp, not sounding very sorry. "In my defense, I thought you'd be away all night."

Derek stiffens. "You didn't invite anyone over, did you?"

I scoff. "I wouldn't do that, Mr. Ledderman."

"I wish you wouldn't call me that," he mumbles, taking off his tie and tossing it on one of the lawn chairs that's set up near the pool.

He sits down on the edge of the lawn chair and I frown, thinking maybe he really is upset.

"I didn't know I wasn't allowed to use the pool," I say in a calm voice, and Derek runs a hand through his hair, leaning down to take off his shoes.

"Who says you weren't?"

His voice sounds a little hoarse.

"Are you okay?" I ask.

Derek offers me a slight smile. "Fine. Just had a couple of drinks at Mom's."

Oh. He's maybe a little tipsy. I've never seen him that way before, and I have to admit that I'm intrigued. Derek is so buttoned-up all of the time and seems to never let loose and have fun.

"I made an extra cocktail if you want it," I say, gesturing to the full glass next to my near empty one. "I planned on having two, but it's probably for the best I don't."

Derek has taken off his shoes and socks and suit jacket, and he stands up in just his slacks and shirt, which he's pulling out of his waistband. He takes the cocktail I'd made and drinks all of it, standing there by the pool.

I blink up at him, still treading water, surprised.

"It's relaxation weekend, right?" he says with a raised eyebrow when I keep looking at him.

I feel my cheeks heat up and I look away.

"You're right. You deserve to relax, Mr. Ledderman."

Derek sighs, rolling his shoulders around as he unbuttons his shirt.

"Stop calling me that," he orders, his voice demanding, and I swallow hard, my heart beating too fast.

"Why?"

"Call me Derek," he commands, without any other explanation, as he takes off his shirt and then his slacks.

I look away, surprised. What's going on with him? He's never this open.

He leaps into the pool, suddenly, in his boxer briefs and

water splashes all over my face. I sputter and dog-paddle, trying to stay afloat.

Derek comes up for air, laughing, his blond hair, sprinkled with silver, slicked back.

"Sorry," he says, but he doesn't seem sorry at all, swimming over to the middle of the pool where I am.

"I'll get out of your hair," I murmur, kicking my legs to swim backward toward the steps, but Derek catches me by one ankle, floating me back over toward him.

"Stay," he says in a low, commanding voice, and now, wild horses couldn't drag me away.

"You're certainly in a mood tonight," I muse, and Derek smiles, tilting his head back so that I can see the line of his throat, his Adam's apple. He looks up at the sunset.

"You told me to relax, and that's what I'm doing," he says. "So, stay in the pool with me and relax, Ms. Lodge."

"You don't have to call me that," I say.

"Kenna," he amends, his voice a low rumble in his chest, and he's staring at me so intensely I'm not quite sure what to do.

What I want to do is wrap my arms around his neck and kiss him, but something tells me that's not what he had in mind tonight.

"I don't have a boyfriend," I blurt out, and Derek freezes for a moment before continuing to tread water.

"I thought you were seeing—"

"I wasn't seeing anyone," I admit, my cheeks burning. "I went out with my female best friend and *her* boyfriend picked us up because we got too drunk."

Derek's face looks blank and then he breaks up, laughing. "Really?"

"Really," I confess miserably. "I guess I just...wanted you to think I had more of a social life."

"Wanted to make me jealous?" he asks, and my eyes shoot to his.

"Did it work?" I ask, surprised at my own boldness.

Derek stares at me for a moment longer.

"Yeah," he says finally in a low tone. "Yeah, it did."

"I'm just the nanny," I murmur.

"Kenna," Derek says, almost like he's scolding me. "You know you're more than that."

"Am I?"

He's looking into my eyes. Derek isn't the best with words. I've been aware of this since I started working for him.

"You must know," he finally says. "You must know that I..."

I swim closer to him, bold enough to wrap my arms around his neck. "Know that you what?"

"How I feel," he starts. "That I'm...attracted to you."

"Is that as far as it goes?" I ask, expecting him not to answer, and in a way, he doesn't. He just shakes his head, biting his bottom lip.

It's me who kisses him, this time, and I can't help myself. I delve my tongue into his mouth. Derek was my first everything. I find myself glad that I had no experience before because I'm sure nothing could have ever topped this feeling.

Derek groans into my mouth, taking my legs and wrapping them around his waist as he continues to tread water.

He kisses me over and over before moving his mouth to my neck, and then he pushes me against the wall of the pool, pressing his hardness against my core.

I moan, tilting my head back to give him more access, and he latches onto the base of my throat, making a mark there.

"There's never been anyone else, Derek," I gasp out.

Derek pulls away, looking at me. "What do you mean?"

I'm blushing fiercely but I figure this is the time to tell him. There will never be a better time. "You were my first," I say, and it has the opposite effect of what I think.

Derek pulls away from me, swimming toward the steps and getting out of the pool.

I pout, pressing my back against the pool wall.

"Derek, can't we just pretend?" I call, unable to help myself. It's desperate and stupid, but I can't stop the words coming out of my mouth. "Just for tonight?"

"Pretend what?" he asks, toweling off his hair and sitting down again on the lawn chair. I climb out of the pool, dripping water and walking over to him. He looks up at me, his head cocked, but he doesn't get up and walk away.

"Pretend that you want me," I say in a shaking voice, straddling his lap. He sits back automatically, his brows furrowed.

"You think that I don't want you?" he breathes.

I tremble as he puts his arms around me, his palms spreading across my bare back. "I don't know what to think."

Derek takes my hand, putting it on the erection that's obvious through his wet boxer-briefs, which cling to him like a second skin.

He groans and rocks his hips up, thrusting into my hand.

"I want you all the time, Kenna," he growls. "I want you so bad it hurts."

"Then why don't you take me?" I ask, my head spinning not from the alcohol but from his nearness, how he smells like sandalwood and chlorine. "I've just been waiting for you to take me."

"Fuck," Derek curses, his green eyes half lidded with lust.

"I want you to. So badly."

I kiss him again, and this time he doesn't pull away.

19

DEREK

Kenna Lodge is driving me fucking crazy. She's rocking her hips against me, kissing along my neck, making these little breathy moans, and I'm harder than diamond beneath her, my hands roving all over her body.

Maybe it's the two whiskeys I had at dinner with my mother. Maybe it's the cocktail that Kenna made. Maybe it's just that I'm drunk on the way she feels and smells and tastes. But I can't do this. I can't give in.

Can I?

She asked me to take her, and it's all I can do not to rip her little bikini off, slide up into her.

"Derek," Kenna whines, her blue eyes glassy with lust. "I want you so badly."

"You're so young," I groan. "You were really a virgin?"

She pouts, sitting up straighter and I grit my teeth as her hot core presses up against the thin layer of fabric between our genitals.

"Does it matter?"

"Of course it fucking *matters*, Kenna. I took something from you. I'm a dirty old man."

"You didn't take it," she argues. "I *gave* it to you. I wanted you to have it. I want you to have me."

"You shouldn't say things like that," I growl, picking her up so that the friction isn't so much. It really has been too long since I've gotten off, and I'm thinking with my dick instead of with my brain.

"I'll say whatever I want to," she says defiantly, turning her chin up.

Fuck. She's cute. She's cute and sexy and she seems all woman in my arms but—

"I'm twenty-two, not seventeen," she complains. "I'm a grown woman and I know what I want, Derek."

"Is that so?" I murmur, and she huffs out a breath, her breasts bouncing in my face. I want so badly to take a nipple into my mouth.

"You're just humoring me," she whines. "You're just teasing me."

I bark out a laugh. "I'm teasing *you*? You're in a string bikini, Kenna, sitting on my lap. Do you know how hard it is not to take you right here and now?"

"Do it," she urges. "I want you to."

"Kenna," I groan. "Are you drunk?"

She shakes her head. "I only had one drink. I know what I want, Derek."

"Do you?" I press up against her and she moans loudly. *God*, she's going to be the death of me. She'd told me to relax, after all. This is supposed to be my vacation. I'm supposed to be able to let loose. "Fuck it," I mumble, and untie her bikini top, Her breasts bounce free and I take a nipple into my mouth, sucking until it pebbles on my tongue.

Kenna breathes out, "Oh, fuck, Derek."

I move my mouth to her other nipple, teasing the first one with my fingertips, and she goes nearly limp, folding over into my arms. I put my arms around her, thrusting up beneath her. This is like being a teenager, dry humping near the pool, but it feels so *good* and I don't know how to stop.

"No one's ever touched you like this?" I ask, nearly breathless. I feel like I could come right now, like a teenager in my underwear.

"No one," she moans. "No one but you, Derek, and it feels so good."

"You like the way I touch you?" I ask, unable to stop asking questions. I love the way she wants only me, the way I'm the only man to have ever made her come.

"I love it," she breathes, looking deep into my eyes. "I think about it when I touch myself."

Heat floods through my body and I grunt and flip her over, covering her body with my own and lying down the lawn chair. I don't know if it's hefty enough to hold our weight, but it's a good thing I purchased the more expensive one, because it might.

Bare breasted, she looks up at me, a flush traveling from her face down between her breasts. I untie the strings of her bottoms, tugging them off and throwing them on the concrete.

"Wish I could taste you again," I grumble, looking down at her sex. She's got a tuft of pubic hair, different than the socialites I've been with who are always waxed bare. I slide my fingers through her lower lips, finding her slick and hot.

Kenna gasps out a breath, arching her back. "Please," she moans.

"Please what?" I ask, smirking slightly as I slide one

finger inside of her. I groan at how she clenches around my finger.

"Please fuck me," she groans, and that's all the push I need.

I spread her thighs roughly and shove down my boxer briefs to slide into her, slowly. I have time to think I should have been gentler, the first time, but Kenna rocks her hips toward me like she wants it rough, harder, and I grit my teeth, trying to get her used to me.

It's not uncommon for women I've been with to be almost too tight to take me. I've always been well-endowed, but Kenna is a whole other thing. She clenches around me like a vice, so sensitive to every stroke.

I start to roll my hips, looking down at her breasts bouncing, at her open mouth, and then I brace myself on one hand and stick two fingers into her mouth. She immediately starts to suck my fingers, and I hum, still moving only my hips.

"Good girl," I praise, and Kenna moans around my fingers. "I'll give you something to do with that mouth soon enough."

She moans again, her breath coming shorter and shorter, and I keep up the pace, knowing that she's close. I keep my teeth gritted, not wanting to come before she does, and when she explodes around me I nearly shout and pull out of her.

"No," Kenna says mournfully, grabbing at my ass to get me closer.

I chuckle. "Told you I'd give you something to do with your mouth, didn't I?"

I've always been a dirty talker in bed, but something about Kenna brings it to another level. She's so sweet and innocent looking, and I can't help wanting to corrupt her.

Kenna sits up, looking suddenly nervous. She shifts to stand up and I sit down on the lawn chair, sitting it back up while she kneels in front of me. I'm pumping myself, my hand slick with her juices, and I'm close already, biting my lip to keep myself from coming.

"I've never done this before," she says in a small voice. "You'll have to teach me."

I frown, looking down at her wide blue eyes. "You don't have to do anything you don't want to do, honey," I say gently, but then Kenna smiles and leans her head forward, slipping me into her mouth. She gags once, twice, and it takes everything in me not to thrust up into her mouth.

"You're doing wonderful, honey," I tell her, and she drags her tongue along the underside of my cock as she takes me deeper, putting her hands on my thighs and digging her fingernails into my flesh.

I reach down to grab her ponytail, popping her off me and groaning at her wide open mouth, her watering eyes.

"I'm going to come," I tell her, gasping out breaths, and Kenna nods, putting her head back down and taking me nearly to my base, using her hand to circle my base.

Instead of moving her head, she hollows her cheeks, sucking hard, and swirls her tongue around me and my vision starts to fade out. It's been so long, and when I explode into her mouth, I thrust up instinctively and Kenna gags again.

"I'm sorry, honey," I murmur, seeing the tears roll down her cheeks, but she's smiling, swallowing, licking her lips.

"You taste good," she says hoarsely, and I pull her up into my lap, my heart beating wildly.

"You're something else, Kenna Lodge," I mumble, kissing along the side of her face.

She giggles, seeming giddy, and wraps her arms around

my neck, her fingers playing in the hair that's gotten too long at the nape of my neck.

I know that I should stop this. I know that I should push her off me, let her down gently, tell her that this is a mistake. She's gotten too close. Too close to my kids, and if I'm honest, too close to me. I'm getting used to seeing her every day, the way she yawns so wide she cracks her jaw in the mornings, how she looks when she's making the kids Mickey Mouse pancakes.

I'm getting in too deep, and I know that this isn't sustainable. She's twenty-two, for God's sake, and she's my employee. Not to mention my ex-wife's niece.

There's so many reasons that this can't happen, and only one reason that I'm letting it. The kids aren't here. It's just us for the weekend, and maybe we *can* pretend for a while.

I feel happier than I have in years, and I don't want to let that go.

Not yet.

20

———

KENNA

I've never been happier in my life. I know that this might not last, that **Derek** can be hot and cold especially when it comes to the two of us hooking up, but this weekend feels...different. His green eyes are warm instead of blank and cold like when he's rejecting me, and we spend hours out by the pool, talking and drinking and kissing.

This is what I want. This is *all* I want, someone like Derek. A family like his. I can't deny to myself anymore that I'm in love with him, and I love his kids just as much. I want to be part of this family, and not just as the nanny.

This is the way to do that, right? Maybe he's considering it too? He's certainly been a lot more open with me than he had been before.

"What's your favorite movie?" I ask, propping myself up on my elbow on one of the lawn chairs, sitting next to Derek. I'm starting to get sleepy from the drink I've had and the late hour, but I don't want to close my eyes. I don't want this to end.

"Big Trouble in Little China," he says without hesitation.

I stare at him. "What's that?"

Derek groans and covers his face with one hand, peeking at me from between his fingers. "You really *are* young."

I laugh and stand up, yawning so widely that my jaw cracks.

Derek's looking up at me, the ghost of a smile on his face. "Tired?"

"A little," I admit with a pout.

"Let's go to bed, then," he murmurs, standing up and toweling himself off. "We can shower in the morning."

I light up. "Together?" I ask hesitantly, and Derek's smile grows wider.

He shrugs. "Fuck it. Why not?"

I squeal and throw my arms around him and he chuckles, shifting to sweep me up in a bridal carry. I promptly put my arms around him, leaning my head on his chest as he carries me into the house and up the stairs. I'm worried for a moment that he'll take me to my bedroom, but he doesn't, kicking open the door of the master bedroom and plopping me down on the bed before closing the door and switching off the lights.

I sleepily undo the ties of my bikini, which are loose anyway from him taking them off so many times. I feel a little achy all over from all the swimming and sex, but it feels good, like after a good workout.

I wiggle under his covers, my hair still damp, but Derek doesn't protest, shucking off his boxers and getting into bed with me.

"Today was the best day," I mutter, and Derek hums in agreement, putting an arm around my waist from behind. I shift, wiggling back against him and he groans.

"Not again."

"Can't keep up, old man?" I taunt, and Derek bites my bare shoulder, making me moan slightly.

"Get some rest, little girl," he growls into my ear and I go limp, smiling, loving the attention.

It's easy to drift off in his arms, even if I expect that he'll be gone when I wake.

He's not, though, instead when I wake up in a few hours, he's wrapped around me like an octopus, one arm around my waist and one leg hooked over my hip. Derek Ledderman, a cuddler. Who would have thought?

I smile but I very badly need to go to the bathroom, so I disentangle myself quickly and Derek makes a displeased, sleepy sound and hugs my pillow instead. I stare down at him for a long moment, ignoring my insistent bladder and watching him. Something swells inside my chest that I can't quite name, but I'm pretty sure it's called love.

I've never been in love before, never even been with a man before Derek, and surely it's unusual to fall for the first man you've ever been with, isn't it?

Maybe I just got lucky.

Derek's master bathroom is twice the size of mine, and I marvel at what appears to be a shower wall in the corner of the big room. I can't wait to shower, feeling the chlorine on my body all sticky. I turn it on and step inside, sighing in relief as the hot water trails down my back from the shower-head. It feels like getting a massage under a waterfall.

I close my eyes as I wet my hair and a smile spreads across my face as I hear footsteps into the room. Derek opens the shower door and steps inside, and I open my eyes, looking at his broad chest, the dusting of blond hair across it.

"Good morning," he says, the sound rumbling in his

chest. I had been afraid that he would be cold to me today, but he's smiling, his green eyes warm.

"Morning," I chirp, my eyes roving over his body as I bite my lip.

Derek blushes, looking away. "I'm glad you like what you see."

"Do you?" I ask, moving my hands away from my breasts. I never knew that I would be this wanton, but I want Derek to see every part of me. I'm not self-conscious because I know that he wants me. At least physically.

The jury is still out on emotionally.

This isn't the time to worry about that, though. I want to spend every second I can with him and I don't want us to talk about anything heavy. Now is the time to just be together, and I'll try to tamp down my hopes for the future.

Derek's green eyes have gone half-lidded with lust as he looks down at me.

"Very much," he murmurs, caging me in with his muscular arms as he puts his hands on the wall behind me. He's a man of few words but I think he makes up for it in action.

He leans his head down to kiss me under the water and he tastes like the fruity drinks I made last night. I sigh happily into his mouth, loving the affection, and Derek moves one hand between my legs, cupping my sex and pressing his thumb up against my clit.

It sends a shock of pleasure up my spine and I gasp, tilting my head back as he moves his lips to my throat, sucking and nipping at the flesh.

I think briefly about whether or not he's used this expensive shower with someone else, but I bat the thought away. I don't want to feel jealousy right now. We're together and that's all that matters. He's here with me now, and I don't care about his past.

And he doesn't have to worry because no one has ever touched me like this before. No one has ever made me *feel* this way before, my muscles loose, my head fuzzy as he puts more pressure on my most sensitive of areas.

He shifts, hooking his index and middle finger inside of me and pressing up in a way I love. I choke out a moan and Derek hums in the back of his throat, a low growling sound that only makes me hotter.

"I want to taste you," he comments, removing his fingers and popping them into his mouth as he looks into my eyes, and I might as well be putty slipping down the shower wall.

Derek kneels and hooks one of my legs around his shoulder, pressing his face against me, his nose bumping against my clit, tongue delving into my entrance.

I let out a long moan and brace one hand on his shoulder, hoping that my legs won't fold when I get closer to my peak.

Derek takes his time, this time, lapping at me slowly, exploring every inch of my lower lips before latching onto my clit and using the same fingers he had before to pump in and out of me.

I groan, getting closer to my orgasm, and I don't know how I'm going to remain standing but somehow I do, my thighs trembling, my breath coming short.

Derek stands up and swiftly turns me around, one hand on my hip the other on my shoulder, until I'm facing the shower wall with my hands braced against it.

He spreads my thighs roughly with one of his before sliding into me, angling up so that I moan out his name and stand up on my tiptoes.

"You're so fucking beautiful," he growls, his voice low and hoarse from sleep.

"Oh, my god," I whisper, not believing that I'm about to be vaulted into another orgasm. All these years not having any and Derek is giving me multiple orgasms each session. I've hit the jackpot with my first lover.

Derek groans and bites down on my shoulder when I tighten around him, coming hard and throwing my head back, and it's only a few more thrusts before I can feel him spilling inside me.

"Now that we've gotten good and dirty, I should clean you up," he comments, and I giggle giddily, handing him the shampoo bottle.

He puts some in his hands to lather and runs his fingers through my hair, rubbing the shampoo into my roots and down to the ends of my hair. It feels almost like a scalp massage and between that and the orgasms and the hot water, it's heaven.

I hum happily as Derek washes and then conditions my hair before focusing on himself, lathering up a loofah and scrubbing his toned body before washing his own hair.

I kiss along his jawline, my tongue darting out to taste the stubble of a growing beard, and Derek laughs.

"That tickles," he scolds, but he's not upset. His eyes are sparkling as he smiles at me.

How can this weekend get any better than this?

21

DEREK

I know that I'm definitely skirting the line of getting in too deep with Kenna. I know that this whole weekend is getting me closer and closer to her, closer to falling for her.

But I just can't seem to help myself. She's so bright and beautiful. I'm realizing that the more time I spend with her, the more I find to like about her. She's funny and smart, too, and she's been so good for my family that I feel in some ways she deserves this.

I feel bad for feeling that way, because I know that Kenna wants more.

Can I give her more?

I don't know. I don't know if that part of my heart will ever be open again, but if it could be open for anyone, it would be Kenna.

She still makes me feel like a dirty old man over the weekend, particularly since she calls Aerosmith "classic rock," but overall, she's mature and well-read.

We talk a *lot* on Saturday.

"Do you have brothers and sisters?" she asks, swinging

her legs on the side of the pool.

I look up at her over my reading glasses. I'd been reading the marketing news, but Kenna in a bikini is far more interesting.

"Only child," I answer.

Kenna nods. "I thought so."

I chuckle. "What does that mean?"

"You just...you like things a certain way," she says vaguely.

"So, I'm uptight?" I ask her.

She turns her head to look at me, grinning. "Maybe a little. Just set in your ways."

"I feel older and older, the longer I spend with you," I tease.

"It's not a bad thing," she says. "I have my own control issues because I *do* have a younger brother and sister. Being the oldest means you make a lot of decisions, and I have a hard time letting others in."

"Is that so?" I ask, thinking that she'd let me in pretty easily.

Kenna blushes. "Maybe not with you."

"So, you'll do what I say?" I ask in a low tone and Kenna blushes harder. It extends all the way down between her breasts and I can't help looking down, licking my lips.

"Maybe sometimes," she hedges, and then looks up at me from under her eyelashes. "In the bedroom, at least."

I smile at her. "A good girl in the sheets and a lady in the streets?"

She laughs. "I don't know about a lady. I'm kind of bossy when I want to be."

"Oh yeah? I would never have guessed," I say dryly. She's certainly been bold about what she wants from me, especially this weekend.

Kenna pouts, pulling her legs out of the water and turning to face me.

"I know what I want. Is that such a bad thing?"

I shake my head. "It's not."

She looks up at me with wide blue eyes. "And you know I want you, Derek," she murmurs, and something stirs in my lower stomach.

I clear my throat, not wanting to have this conversation right now. "You've got me," I say idly.

"For the weekend," she points out.

"For the weekend," I agree, looking back at my newspaper as Kenna lets out a frustrated breath.

"Why not longer?" she asks.

"Because things are complicated."

"Why are they complicated?" She scoots closer to my lawn chair, propping her feet up on the bottom of it.

I look at her incredulously. "So many reasons, Kenna. You have to know that."

"Because I'm Suzanna's niece?"

"Because you're *twenty-two*."

She huffs again. "What does *that* have to do with anything?"

"How old do you think I am?" I ask.

Kenna's quiet for a moment. "I don't know. Thirty, thirty-two?"

"Thirty-*eight*," I say flatly. "I was in high school when you were born."

She just looks at me. "So what? Lots of people have age gaps. Hell, my mom is ten years younger than my dad."

"Ten years isn't sixteen years," I point out.

She shakes her head. "I just don't think it's that big of a deal."

"Maybe not," I sigh. "But you're also my employee, and

generally that's frowned upon."

Kenna scoffs. "It's not like we work in some corporate office."

"No, it's worse. You take care of my kids."

"I love your kids."

"I know," I say softly, and take in a deep breath before standing up.

Kenna sits up straight, something like panic in her blue eyes. "Derek, I'm sorry, please don't—"

I turn to look at her. "Please don't what? I'm just going to make us some lunch."

She breaks out into a big smile. "Oh."

Kenna follows me into the kitchen as I make us some roast beef sandwiches, toasting the bread and melting some Swiss cheese on the meat.

She has a mouthful of sandwich when she moans. "How did you learn to cook so well?"

I snort. "This isn't exactly cooking, but I learned after Suzanna left. The kids don't really like fast food, so I sort of had to."

"Well, you're really good at it," she praises. "All I can make are pancakes."

"Delicious Mickey Mouse pancakes," I correct her.

Kenna laughs. She's been laughing a lot this weekend, and she looks so pretty when she laughs. I look away, my heart beating too hard.

"I do my best. Been around kids most of my life. My sister is ten years younger."

I smile. "She must have been a surprise for your mother."

"You have no idea," Kenna says, picking a spear of pickle off my plate.

"You little thief," I mutter, and she crunches the pickle,

smiling. God, she's cute. I don't think I've had this much fun in a weekend.... well, maybe ever. Certainly not since high school, when I had less responsibilities and more fun.

Panic starts to rise in my throat, my heart pounding, but I try to push it down, try to ignore it. I clear my throat and look down at the sandwich I've nearly finished.

"What do you want to do next?" Kenna asks excitedly, and I grin at her.

"We're watching Big Trouble in Little China."

She groans. "That sounds like such a *guy* movie."

"What's that supposed to mean?"

Kenna looks at me. "You know, lots of action, no real plot."

"That's what's wonderful about it. You'll see."

She gives me a sly smile. "Do we get to cuddle on the couch?"

"Naturally."

She pops up from her seat. "Then I'm in."

Kenna is dozing cuddled up under my arm before all the characters are introduced. I could wake her up, but I'm watching her, the way she's snoring lightly, her full mouth parted. Her eyelashes fan out over her cheekbones, her eyelids fluttering like she's dreaming.

My chest feels tight.

I've got to end this. I've got to get back to what's important: Maggie and Eli. I can't lose my heart again. I can tell myself that it's because of the kids all I want. I can tell myself that I don't want Kenna to leave and abandon the kids but what I'm *really* afraid of is that I'll let myself fall and she'll leave *me*. Abandon *me*.

I can't handle that again.

So, I let myself watch Kenna sleep, because this is the last few hours we have to pretend.

22

———

KENNA

I'm sure that Derek has no idea what this means to me. I don't even know what it means to him. It could mean nothing. It could mean that he's just giving in for the fun of it, just because he wants my body, not my heart.

I know that I want more. I've told him as much, in my own words, but it just now occurs to me that he hasn't wanted to talk about it.

When I wake up, I've shifted to have my head in his lap on the couch and I turn over, smiling, but my smile fades quickly because there's something different in his face. He doesn't look carefree like he's looked all weekend. He doesn't look...happy. He looks concerned, his expression blank but his brows slightly furrowed.

"What's wrong?" I ask, and Derek offers me that charming half smile.

"Nothing at all," he soothes, smoothing down my hair, leaning down to kiss my forehead. It's all very sweet and just like he's been acting all weekend, but something's changed.

I don't want it to change. I don't want anything to change. I sit up, trying not to frown.

What happens now? Is this when we get together? I don't know how to talk to him about it. I've never been in this situation before. I've never met a man like him before. I've never had to talk about a *relationship* and what that means for me or for him.

I feel small and desperate and stupid, but I also feel my heart swell every time he looks at me. I don't know where to go from here. I open my mouth to ask him – ask him....what?

Before I can ask or stumble over my words or shut my mouth again, whatever I'm about to do, he kisses me, and I forget what I was going to say. I forget everything the second his tongue touches mine, just like always.

Before I know what's happening, he has me on my back, my ankles at his shoulders, and he's pressing into me and leaning down to kiss me over and over. And this isn't different. This part is the same, the way he looks into my eyes. It's like we're the only people in the world. Sex can't always be like this, right? This intense? This...good?

I've heard my friends talk about it and it didn't seem like this.

"Derek," I gasp out. "Derek, I—"

"Hmm?" he murmurs, looking down at where he's pumping in and out of me.

I bite my tongue to not tell him that I love him, just sighing out a moan and coming hard around him when he keeps thrusting into me.

"You slept through my favorite movie," he says after he's spilled inside of me and we're lying on the couch, him spooning me, his arms around my waist.

I tuck the back of my head against his shoulder. "Sorry," I murmur.

The truth is, I've been exhausted over the last few weeks. I think it was all the stress from the court and our back and forth. I'm not quite recovered yet. But I don't want Derek to know that. I don't want to bother him with it, more like it. I feel like I'm on this precipice with Derek, like if I take a wrong turn, he might run.

It's strange to think of a strong alpha male like Derek as skittish, but when it comes to matters of the heart, I feel like he is. After all, I have to think about what my aunt did to him. I have to think about how that must have broken him in ways I can't understand.

"Do you have regrets?" I ask, and I guess I mean, does he regret marrying Aunt Suzanna, but that's not how he answers.

"Everyone has regrets."

"You know what I mean," I hedge.

"Don't know if I do." His voice is low and smooth, like he doesn't have a care in the world.

I wonder if I'm overthinking this.

"I only regret things I *didn't* do," I say.

He grunts. "Like all those guys you didn't sleep with in high school?"

I giggle. "Some of them," I say, wiggling back against him.

Derek grabs my hip tightly and leans down to bite my shoulder, making me moan. He pulls away, seeming satisfied.

"I don't regret *that*," I continue. "It's more the things I didn't do. All the parties I never attended."

He scoffs. "You think I went to parties?"

I twist my head around to look at him. "Didn't you?"

Derek shrugs. "A couple, I guess, with Grayson and Loxton. But they're stupid parties. Especially rich people parties."

I grin. "Rich people parties? Aren't you a rich person?"

"Yeah, now," he says. "I wasn't always."

I frown. "Your parents, they didn't have money?"

"Not like Grayson or Loxton," he says.

"They're your friends?" I ask, enamored by him. He never talks this much, and I'm eating every word up.

"I grew up with them. Well, mostly. I'm a few years older, but I never much hung around with kids from high school or anything. I guess Logan and I were close, and Grayson and Loxton were. It was just the way things were."

"Back in the Paleolithic Era?" I joke.

Derek groans. "Don't remind me."

"I can't even *imagine* you in high school," I admit. Derek seems like he's always been this way, always been this stubborn, always looked just like this with gray in his hair and his jaw set, seeming so intimidating until he smiles.

"That's because you were a fetus when I was in high school," he pokes at my hip with one finger, making me twist because it's ticklish.

I shift so that I can face him, brushing my nose against his. Derek doesn't move away, and it encourages me.

"Is that when you met my aunt?" I ask softly, and for a long moment he doesn't answer and I think he won't answer.

Derek finally just nods.

"Was there ever anyone else?" I ask, not sure what I want the answer to be.

"Not really. Here and there, but mostly after she left."

"So, she was your first," I say, and some part of me hates it. Some part of me hates that he was with her and especially hates what she did to him. But I guess if she hadn't, I wouldn't be here, and I wouldn't be this happy.

"Doesn't matter," he mutters.

"You think your first doesn't matter?"

"Not if you don't let it matter," he says matter-of-factly, and I frown, feeling almost offended. I don't know how to express myself without sounding like some little girl with a crush, though, so I keep my mouth shut.

I want to enjoy this, and we have one more kid-free night, so I'm not going to make him answer the hard questions if he doesn't want to.

"I would offer to make dinner, but I'm sure you're pretty tired of Mickey Mouse pancakes," I tease, trying to lighten the mood.

Derek snorts. "How about we just order pizza?"

My eyes light up. I know I probably shouldn't eat so much; I'll get bloated, but at the same time, I haven't been self-conscious once with Derek. He's just got a way about him that makes me feel beautiful. Besides, I'm hungry. Not to mention I *love* pizza.

"Extra olives," I say excitedly as he orders. "Don't forget the olives."

Derek looks at me like I'm nuts. "Olives?"

I shrug. "Just craving them," I say, and he shrugs and orders a large pepperoni with extra olives and some garlic bread.

I climb into his lap while he's on the phone and he chuckles, putting his arms around me while he finishes ordering. I'm still just wearing one of his T-shirts, and by the time the pizza delivery guy gets there, we're making out on the couch, his hand trailing along my inner thigh.

Derek groans when the doorbell rings.

"I'll get it," I offer, standing up, but he grabs the hem of his T-shirt and tugs me back down on the couch, frowning.

"Not with your ass hanging out," he barks, and I grin up at him. I like it when he gets possessive, I can't help myself. I watch him adjust himself in his sweats as he goes to the door and my heart just nearly leaps out of my chest. It's amazing, how much you can want someone that you barely know, really.

Derek doesn't open up, or at least he hasn't until this weekend, but when the pizza arrives, he drinks a few beers even though I decline, not wanting to blur any other part of this weekend with booze, and as I see it, nothing can happen that will ruin this weekend for me.

23

DEREK

I probably drink too much after the pizza comes. That's what I blame it on, later, I blame it on the booze and the rare weekend without my kids and my vacation. I blame it on everything else but my heart.

I don't remember, later, what moment it was that made me lose it. I don't remember why. Something about the way she smiled or how she ate her pizza, something about how she looked at me.

"Kenna," I say, and she turns toward me with the biggest smile. "Look at you."

Kenna looks down at herself as if something like pizza has fallen on her T-shirt and I laugh.

"What?" she asks, and I shake my head, smiling, as if I'm not sure, either. She pouts when I don't answer, crawls across the floor where she's been sitting cross-legged and puts her hands on my thighs. "You can't close up on me now, not the last night."

I take in a deep breath, looking down into her bright blue eyes.

"A guy could fall in love," I mumble, and Kenna climbs

up into my lap and kisses me until I pick her up and carry her up the stairs.

We don't even make it halfway. I take her right there, on the stairs, and it's uncomfortable and we'll probably both have bruises but I just cannot *wait* to have her. I never had that with Suzanna, or the brief flings that I had since Suzanna left. I never had that with *anybody*.

I can't keep my hands off her, all weekend, and I have no idea how we turn back from this. I don't want to, and it scares the absolute shit out of me.

I slide my hands up the T-shirt that she's wearing, *my* T-shirt, and she arches her back as I pump in and out of her as she cries out my name, and I love the sound of it on her tongue. I kiss her like I can taste it there and she mumbles something into my mouth.

I pull away so that I can hear her, looking into her eyes, and that's when my heart stops beating.

I can see it in her eyes. I can see it all over her face and part of me is hoping she'll say it and another part knows that if she does, we can't ever go back.

"I'm already in love with you, Derek," she says, her voice cracking, and there are tears in her eyes and my heart is soaring and breaking at the same time.

I did this. I did this to her, and I can't back it up. I can't tell her that I love her too because I'm too scared and broken to know if I can love her back in the way she deserves.

But I can't tell her any of that so I just kiss her, angle my hips up like I've discovered she likes, and she clenches around me, coming, clawing her nails down my shoulders.

I hope it stings for days in the shower.

When we're both spent, I pick her up and she's light as a feather. Her arms go around my neck and she tucks her head against my chest. I put her in my bed again, unable to face putting her back in her own. Not yet, anyway.

She nuzzles up against me and my breath catches in my throat.

"Do you think you could love me too, Derek?" she murmurs.

My heart seizes up in my chest and I tell myself not to speak, not to say anything.

"Maybe I already do," I murmur back, and Kenna doesn't push me. She doesn't say anything, just rests her head on my chest and closes her eyes.

I don't sleep for hours and hours, staring at the ceiling and trying to figure out what the fuck I'm going to do.

THE KIDS AREN'T COMING BACK until the afternoon, or at least that's what my mother said, but I have a sneaking suspicion she'll bring them back early. They can be more than a handful, and my mother's getting up there in age. She has some trouble with arthritis and that's why she can't watch them full-time.

So, I get up early, leave Kenna snoring softly in my bed, still in just my T-shirt, and make a pot of coffee. I still have no idea how I'm going to walk this back. I don't know how I'm going to do this, after this weekend.

It turns out that I don't have much time to think about it, because I hear the buzz of the gate opening through the intercom and I squeeze my eyes shut tight.

Maggie comes running in through the back door to the kitchen wearing a princess dress and with a tiara tangled in her hair. "Daddy, Daddy look," she says, holding up a wand that has seen better days. "Nana got me a wand!"

"You're a real princess," I say, smiling down at her, and then my mother walks in, holding Eli on her hip.

She looks exhausted and I take him from her. He plants a big kiss on my cheek and rests his head on my shoulder, seeming almost as tired as my mother does.

Maggie's all energy, though, waving around her wand and shouting and then she runs into the living room and lets out a big gasp as I'm telling Mom goodbye.

"You had *pizza* without us?"

I groan inwardly, remembering that I haven't cleaned up after last night.

I smile at my mother. "Thank you for watching them this weekend," I say, and lean down to kiss her cheek.

"We had a blast," she says, smiling back, and pats my shoulder. "I'm going home to lie down," she says dryly, and I laugh.

"See you next time, Mom."

I trail into the living room with Eli. I plop him down on the couch and he lies down, sucking his thumb. I sigh. I've really got to work on breaking him of that before his teeth grow in crooked.

One hurdle at a time.

Maggie frowns up at me, gesturing down to the pizza box and I laugh.

"I'll order you guys some tonight," I promise, and she finally favors me with a smile.

Eli seems half asleep and I know that I'll have to get him up and started again if I want him to sleep tonight, but he looks so cute there on the couch that I can't quite bring myself to do it.

"Did you have fun, buddy?" I ask softly, and Eli smiles around his thumb, nodding.

He keeps looking toward the stairs. Maggie's still looking

at the pizza as if I've betrayed her. It feels strange to have been without them for two full nights and a day, and it's like I didn't realize until this moment how much I've missed them.

I sit down on the couch next to Eli, feeling almost exhausted myself after a debaucherous weekend that I can never repeat.

Kenna comes down the stairs, and thank god she's pulled on a pair of my sweats. She rubs her eyes and blinks once or twice, standing on the stairs and I can barely bear to look at her.

Eli pops off the couch suddenly, startling me, and goes running full-tilt toward the stairs.

"*Mama!*" he shouts, jumping up into Kenna's arms, and my heart seems to drop out of my body into the floor.

24

KENNA

I look over at Derek, shocked, and there's absolutely nothing on his face. It's like he's shut off all over again and my heart sinks.

I hug Eli tightly, kissing along the side of his face. It's not like this is the first time a kid has tripped up and called me "mom," in the years that I've spent volunteer teaching at college and babysitting.

But it means something to Derek, and watching him shut down proves that to me.

Eli falls asleep in my arms and I notice that he's a little warm, but I chalk it up to the sunny day outside and the car ride here. I lie him back down on the couch and Derek clears his throat, starting to clean up the pizza boxes and glasses we had left lying around.

Something's changed since this weekend and I can feel it, but I know that Derek won't want us to tell the kids that we're together. Not yet, anyway. It's complicated.

I shouldn't be worried.

Right?

Maggie and I go into her room to play princesses and

she finds me a tiara out of her toy box and a wand that's bent in the middle. I don't complain and grin at her and we play for a long while. In the back of my head, I'm thinking about this weekend and about Derek, but I let myself let loose with Maggie and have fun with her for a little bit.

When I get out into the hallway, Derek has Eli in his arms, taking him to the bedroom.

"Gonna let him nap for a while?" I ask.

Derek nods tersely. "He seems tired from the trip. They must have played pretty hard this weekend."

I smile. "So did we," I whisper, but Derek doesn't crack a smile, just walking into Eli's room.

I wait there in the hallway for him to come out, but he doesn't, and I sigh and walk down to grab myself a coffee. I'm still wearing his clothes, for god's sake. I should change, but I can't bring myself to, not yet. They smell like him.

Some part of me knows that this weekend might have been a one-time thing but the rest of me? It's filled with so much hope that I can barely stand it.

Derek stays upstairs for a long time, and Maggie's playing by herself in her bedroom and Eli's sleeping and I don't know what to do with myself.

I just sit down at the table, waiting for Derek, and I feel stupid but it's all I can do.

Derek finally comes back downstairs and he sits across from me at the table. "Kenna," he says, and he won't look at me.

Don't, I want to say. *Derek, don't.*

But I know if I speak I'm going to cry so I just look down at the table.

"I can't do this," he says, his tone low so the kids won't hear.

I just nod, tears brimming in my eyes.

"If you want to take the day off..." he says, trailing off, and I get up suddenly, sliding on a pair of my flip-flops that I've left near the door and grabbing my purse.

I stop at the door, looking back at him. His shoulders are slumped and I will him to look at me, just once, even though tears are streaming down my face, but he doesn't.

I take in a shaky breath and all but run to my car in the garage, unable to fight my tears.

I sit in the car for what seems like forever before I crank it up and back out of there. I sniffle and make it another two miles before I have to pull over, sobbing as if my heart is shredded into a thousand pieces.

Is this a broken heart? Is this what it feels like? Because if so, I don't think I want to be in love.

I call the only person I can think of: Cherie.

"Hey, girl," she answers brightly.

"Cherie," I croak.

"Oh no, Kenna, what happened?" she asks, but I just sob into the phone.

"Come over," she insists. "Right now."

Luckily, Cherie lives nearby with her boyfriend, and I make it there without killing myself and I've mostly stopped crying when I arrive.

I'm so glad that her boyfriend's car isn't in the driveway. I don't think I could deal with any men today. Not after all this.

Cherie pulls me into a hug as soon as I walk through the door and I hug her back tightly, feeling slightly better already. There are certain things only a best friend can fix.

"Tell me everything," she says, and I spill it all, crying a little toward the end. When I'm done, she blinks at me, her brown eyes wide.

"That *ass*," she seethes. "How dare he?"

"It's not like that," I complain tiredly, slumping down on her couch, lying my head on the couch arm. I tell her about Eli, what he'd called me when he ran up to me.

"That happens, though," she argues, but I know that it's different for those kids. I could try to explain it but I'm just so exhausted emotionally and physically from the intense weekend.

"I don't know what to do," I say in a liquid voice, and then, suddenly, my stomach rolls and saliva fills my mouth and I know that I'm going to be sick. I barely make it to the restroom and Cherie follows me, standing just outside the door. When I open it, she takes my hand.

"Kenna," she says slowly. "How long have you been sick?"

"I've been tired and had a few dizzy spells," I tell her. "But I haven't been sick. I'm sure it's just the stress. It's too much."

Cherie bites her lip. "I'm sure it is. Just curious, anyway. When was the last time you had your period?"

I frown at her. "What's that got to do with—" I start, and then Cherie keeps staring at me and slowly, my eyes widen. "Wait."

"I have tests," she says quickly, as if that's supposed to make me feel better. Panic rises in my throat as I wrack my brain trying to think of the last time I've menstruated. It's been longer than a month. Oh god, when was it? I've just been so busy with the kids and all this with Derek....

"It's not possible," I whisper, and Cherie raises an eyebrow.

"Did you use protection?"

"Shit," I curse, and Cherie sighs and pats my shoulder.

"It could be just stress. Nine times out of ten it is," she assures me. "But we better take one to be safe."

She pulls out a grocery bag full of tests and I gape at her.

She shrugs. "You live with someone, sometimes you forget protection," she defends herself, and I guess I'm not one to judge. I hadn't even *thought* about protection.

To my credit, this is the first time I've ever been with anyone.

She hands me a test and I just stare at it.

"That's not how you use it," she says gently, and I bark out a laugh.

"I don't know if I can take it," I say honestly, looking up at her.

Cherie looks empathetic. "I understand. I've been there," she says. "But I'm telling you, it's probably going to be negative and then you'll feel so much better."

"Good," I say, calming down a little. "Because I *can't* be pregnant."

Five minutes later, I'm standing in the doorway of the bathroom, looking at the back of the toilet where the test is sitting.

"Do you want me to check it?" Cherie asks, and I shake my head.

"I can do this," I mutter. It'll be negative. It'll definitely be negative. I feel a sense of peace come across my body, having convinced myself that Cherie is right, and I pick up the test gingerly and look down at it, taking a deep breath.

It's one of those simple ones, that just says pregnant or not pregnant in the indicator window.

I blink about ten times, thinking that it'll change, but it doesn't.

Pregnant.

25

DEREK

"Where's Kenna?" Maggie asks about half an hour after Kenna leaves, and it feels like a little stab in my heart.

"Taking time off," I tell her. "We talked about this."

Maggie pouts up at me. "Sorry," she mumbles.

I want to kick myself. I'm being snappy with my six-year-old because I can't handle my own emotions, and it's not fair.

I lean down and kiss the crown of her head. "No, baby, I'm sorry. Daddy's just...tired."

"I'm tired *too*," she whines. "And I want pizza."

I chuckle. "Will you forgive me if I order pizza?"

"Extra cheese."

My daughter has just angled a bribe out of me, but I can't bring myself to care after everything that's gone on this morning.

"Fair enough."

I order the pizza and Eli wakes up, coming downstairs and climbing into my lap on the couch while we watch Paw

Patrol. The kids have been better about screentime but I'm too emotionally exhausted to make them turn it off.

Sometimes parents need a break, and since I've just had a weekend off, I shouldn't, but here I am.

Maggie and Eli are quiet the rest of the evening, which I'm not sure is a good thing. I'm just left alone with my thoughts, and my thoughts are not a good place to be.

They eat and get bathed and when I'm reading Eli a story, he pouts just a little.

"I know Kenna does it differently," I say. "She'll be back soon."

Eli looks at me with his big green eyes and I think maybe he'll throw a tantrum, but he doesn't, just lying down and pulling the covers up.

I frown, wondering if he might be coming down with something, but I know he's had a long weekend. Haven't we all?

Maggie is already asleep when I leave Eli's room, still holding the wand her Nana got her.

Now, I'm *really* left alone with my thoughts.

I walk into my office, planning to try and do some work, email some potential clients, but I just end up staring at the blinking cursor.

What have I done?

I've played with Kenna's emotions, and had my fun with her, and then just discarded her? Is this the kind of man I want to be?

I sigh and rub my hands across my face. Will Kenna even come back, after everything? Eli's calling her "mama," and they're so attached that I can't imagine having to explain to them that's she's gone forever.

All because of me.

I don't sleep that night.

I'm sitting at the kitchen table around daylight when I hear the gate buzz. I sit straight up, clearing my throat, as Kenna comes into the back door of the kitchen.

She doesn't even look at me, just walks upstairs to her room, shutting the door softly behind her. I know that I need to talk to her. I know that I need to explain things, explain *why* I can't do this, but right now, I can't bring myself to do it.

I head to work and fall asleep during a presentation one of the junior marketing executives is giving, and Grayson pulls me into his office after, shutting the door behind me.

"What's going on with you?" he asks.

"I'm sorry," I apologize. "I didn't sleep last night."

Grayson frowns. "Well, go home, old man," he teases, and I glare at him.

"I want to work," I say.

"More like you're afraid to go home," Grayson drawls.

I groan. "How do you know that?"

"I've been friends with you long enough to know something's up," Grayson says. "Is it still that pretty young nanny?"

"I did something stupid, Grayson," I admit.

He just looks at me. "That's not really like you."

"I don't know what's like me anymore," I grumble.

I'm not much for talking about my personal life, even with my best friends, but Grayson is a good friend, and I need *someone* to talk to since I can't talk to Kenna.

Grayson sits down in his desk chair and I plop down on the chair. I spill out everything about the weekend and what Eli had done this morning.

"You need a drink," he points out, and I bark out a laugh.

"Maybe I do," I mutter.

"Call your nanny and tell her you'll be home late," he says, but I shake my head.

"I can't talk to her."

"Pussy," Grayson taunts. "You've got to work with her, right? No matter what happens between you, you can't take her away from those kids."

I sigh. "I guess you're right, but I'm not ready."

Grayson runs a hand through his hair and picks up his phone, texting someone.

"I told Lilian that we're day-drinking. We're taking the afternoon off and we're going to the Dive," my friend says firmly.

THE DIVE IS near-empty other than the barflies that are permanent fixtures on the stools.

It takes me two drinks before I can even talk about Kenna.

"Do you love her?" Grayson asks me, looking right at me.

I swallow hard, my words catching in my throat.

"I don't know," I admit. I know that I'm close. I know that losing my heart is a real possibility and I never thought this would happen for me again, but I don't know if I can say it.

"Don't you?" Grayson asks softly.

"Fuck," I curse, looking down at my drink. "I didn't know it could happen for me again, Grayson."

"But it did," he points out, and I look back up at him.

"It did," I admit. It's the first time I've admitted it, even to myself, but ever since the first time I saw Kenna with the kids, ever since the first time I kissed her, I think I started to fall.

"And you know she feels the same."

"Do I?" I think about it, how she told me she loved me, but at the same time, I'm her first. How does she even know what love is?

"Just because she's young doesn't mean that she doesn't know her own heart, Derek."

"Suzanna said she loved me, too," I mumble, and Grayson sighs.

"I understand how it feels to shut your heart off, you know?" he says, and he's right, he does. He'd done the same when Lilian left, before she came back.

"I don't know how to get it back," I confess, ordering another drink.

"Neither did I," Grayson says with a chuckle. "But it turns out that you can."

"I don't know if *I* can," I insist, and I'm being stubborn but I'm also telling the truth. The only way I knew how to handle what Suzanna did was shutting everything down. I hadn't talked about it unless I was drunk, hadn't dealt with it unless I had to.

My friend shrugs. "You'll have to figure out if she's worth it."

I'm silent because the thing is, I know that she is.

I just don't know that I am.

It's another four drinks (five?) before Lilian comes to pick us up and drives me back home, and I don't feel like I've made any progress in feeling better. At least I feel numb in a way, the alcohol fuzzing out the harshest parts of what I feel, but still, all I can think about is Kenna.

It's only nine in the evening when I arrive, and I know that I'm late but I couldn't bring myself to call her ahead of time.

I expect her to be in bed, but instead when I stumble

inside and kick off my shoes, she's sitting in the living room and she stands up.

"Where have you been?" she hisses. "I was worried sick."

I look down at my phone and see that I have about a dozen missed calls.

"Shit," I say thickly, and Kenna tilts her head.

"Are you...drunk?"

I nod slowly, looking at her, and she sighs.

"Derek," she says, but it's not scolding, more like almost soft. "Can't we talk about this?"

"Talk about what?" I ask, sitting down heavily on the couch and loosening my tie.

Kenna doesn't back down. "You know what."

I shrug, the alcohol making it seem like this is easier to deal with even though my heart is still aching.

"There's nothing to talk about," I say firmly, and Kenna nods tersely.

"Okay," she says tightly. "Fine." She pauses. "But the next time you're going to be three hours late, you better call me. I might have somewhere else to be."

My gaze snaps to hers and I feel something like jealousy brewing in my stomach. It's stupid. She's told me that she's not seeing anyone else, but aren't all bets off now?

"What's that supposed to mean?"

"None of your business," she snaps, and stalks up the stairs.

Great. I really handled that well.

"Kenna," I call after her, and she turns.

"What do you want from me, Derek?" she asks, sounding exasperated, her face stricken.

I swallow hard, and look away.

"You're too young," I mumble.

"You're starting to sound like a broken record," she snaps, and continues up the stairs.

The sound of her shutting her door is loud in my head, and I end up falling asleep on the couch, trying to run from my thoughts.

26

KENNA

I spent last night at Cherie's house, talking with her all night, and I'd barely slept. It seems like I won't sleep tonight, either, because of how furious I am with Derek.

Cherie is right. How dare he? He spent the whole weekend open with me, making love to me, and now it's just over? Just because what? Because I'm twenty-two instead of thirty-two?

I know my own mind and my own emotions. I'm a grown woman. I pace around my room, unable to settle down, but finally, I sit on the edge of my bed.

I expect to hear Derek clomping up the stairs, but I don't, and finally, I manage a thin few hours of sleep.

When I wake up, Derek and the kids are gone, and he's left me a note.

Take the day off.

I fume. The only reason he's taking the kids to that drop-in daycare or his parents' house is because he's afraid to be here alone with me.

I don't know what to do. I want to tell him about the

baby growing in my stomach, but he won't even talk to me. Am I supposed to ambush him and just blurt it out? That sounds childish and selfish. He needs to be told, but what future can we have if he doesn't even think I'm adult enough to be with? Will he ask me to terminate it because I'm not old enough to be a mom?

Thinking about all of this is making me so stressed I want to throw up again.

First things first. I need to know if everything is okay. Regardless of what will happen when I tell Derek, I already know I'm keeping this baby, so I have to see a doctor and then I can figure out where to go from there.

With a plan in mind, I call around and manage to get an appointment to see a doctor. All the times I'd imagined having kids, I never thought that I would be going to an ultrasound alone, but here I am.

Derek is not a possibility, with his silent treatment right now. Mom and Dad would be delighted under normal circumstances, but these circumstances are all but normal. I know that Cherie would have gone with me, but I don't want to ask her. I figure, worst case scenario, if I'm going to have to raise this baby alone, I might as well do the appointment alone.

I think that I'll be okay. I don't feel like crying, that is, until the doctor puts the ultrasound inside my vagina, and I hear the heartbeat.

It's steady and strong and I instantly burst into tears.

The doctor looks at me. "There are options..." she starts, but I cut her off, shaking my head.

"It's just happiness," I insist, although it's certainly mixed with sadness. "I've always wanted a baby."

She smiles. "It looks like you're around ten weeks along.

The baby seems to be doing well. Just make sure that you up your calorie intake a little bit each week."

"I'll have no trouble doing that," I state with a snort.

When I get back to Derek's mansion, I stare at the ultrasound pictures and I wonder how in the hell I'm going to tell my parents. For all they know, I never even had a boyfriend. I don't know how to tell them that I've been sleeping with my boss.

I *can't* tell them. I can't tell anyone. Cherie knows, but I know that she won't say anything. Derek needs to know, of course, but he needs to be around and willing to talk to me first.

I don't know what to do, if I'm honest. How will I be able to continue working with him and being around those two kids I love like my own already, while I have to worry about my little one too? And will he ever talk to me again? I need to tell him , but how? Will he wait months? Will I be showing by then?

My stomach turns and I run to the bathroom. Since I didn't eat anything yet, nothing but bile comes out. All this stress is making me sick, literally. And it's bad for the baby.

As I realize the options I have, tears start streaming down my face. Because there is really no choice at all to be made. There's only one solution.

I have to quit.

It breaks my heart, because I truly have grown to love Eli and Maggie, and I don't know how I'm going to go on without them in my life.

Maggie and her unicorns and princesses, the way she so proudly shows me her drawings, knowing that I'll praise them. Eli and his trains and the sweet way he smiles at me. His little voice, calling me "mama."

It physically hurts to think about leaving them, but I

don't know what else to do.

Derek won't talk to me, and I can't hurt my baby any more. He needs to know he's about to be a dad again, but how do I tell him?

He says I'm too young, yet he is the one playing games and hiding from me. I can't do this anymore. I know how I feel. I know I'd give him forever if he just said the word, but all he does is play with my feelings.

I may be young, but I'm not dumb. It's clear he wants my body, but not my heart. And I need more. I need to take care of this baby inside me and make sure he or she is okay. The baby is the most important person in my world right now. Him or her and the two little angels I've been loving, Maggie and Eli. But unfortunately their dad is making me choose and I need to give this little one a fighting chance. So, I have to go. Distance myself from what hurts me the most. Derek.

I tell myself that I'll tell him that I'm leaving the second that he gets home, but I pass out in my bed, surrounded by ultrasound pictures.

I wake up three hours later because someone's standing next to my bed. I startle and then I sit up to see Eli standing there, swaying slightly. At first, I think he's just sleepy, but when I pick him up, I realize that he's burning up with a fever.

"Eli," I soothe, patting his hair.

"Mama," he whines, tucking his face into my shoulder, and my heart aches.

I want to be his mama. I want Derek and I want Eli and Maggie and I want this baby. I want this family, but Derek thinks I'm not old enough. Not good enough.

I can't think about that right now though. Worried about Eli, I knock on Derek's door. I don't care if he doesn't talk to me about us, but Eli needs him right now.

He sits straight up in bed. "What's wrong?"

"It's Eli," I whisper. "He's burning up."

I hand him off to Derek and go to wake up Maggie, knowing that a trip to the emergency room might be near.

Derek looks pale when he comes into the living room. "It's a hundred and three," he says, and I rush Maggie out to the car, buckling her in her seat while she still dozes.

Derek buckles in a crying Eli, and it doesn't even occur to me to stay home. I need to be there. I need to know that Eli's all right.

The car is silent other than the sound of Eli's crying and me trying to soothe him, turned around and patting his thigh, holding his hand.

"It's gonna be okay, buddy," I tell him in a gentle voice.

"I don't feel good," he sobs.

"I know. The doctor is going to make you feel better," I assure him.

Derek glances at me and I glance at him and we're both terrified. I've never seen Eli sick, and from Derek's reaction, I don't think he's been this sick before.

When we arrive at the hospital, I take Maggie out and kiss her forehead, checking her for a fever, but she's fine. She sleeps in my arms while we wait, and I stay with her out in the lobby while Derek takes Eli back to see the doctor, my heart pounding in my chest.

It takes hours before Derek returns, but I can't sleep despite trying to get comfortable. He returns looking almost gray, his face stricken.

"What's wrong?" I ask in a half-whisper, not wanting to wake Maggie.

"They don't know," he says, his voice breaking. He sits down hard on the chair next to me. "They think it could be meningitis."

I gasp. "But Maggie isn't sick." I know that meningitis is horribly contagious.

"What if it's bacterial?" Derek asks hoarsely, and my mouth goes dry.

Bacterial meningitis is one of the first things I learned about in the classes I took about common childhood illnesses. It's very commonly fatal.

"They don't know that yet," I assure him, putting a hand on his shoulder. I expect him to pull away with how cold and harsh he's been with me since the kids got home, but instead, he leans into me. No matter what I have going on, even with the baby growing in my belly, I need to be here for Derek, Maggie, and Eli. And no matter how much he needs to know, now is not the time. This time is about Eli and getting him better. My baby is fine for now, so there is no harm in waiting a little bit longer.

"I've got Maggie, if you need to go back in," I tell him, and Derek looks up at me with tears in his eyes.

"He's calling for Mama," he says hoarsely, and I swallow hard. "Give me Maggie," he says, taking her from me. "He needs you."

My heart skips several beats but I walk to the back, asking the nurse station which room Eli is in. He's still in a room in the emergency room, and he seems in and out of consciousness.

I sit next to him, talking to him softly and holding his hand, until he falls asleep. I doze off too, in the uncomfortable chair.

When I wake, I go back out to the waiting room to see Derek asleep with Maggie in his arms. I tap his shoulder.

"Want to switch?" I ask, and Derek groans.

"My arms are asleep," he admits, handing her over and shaking them out.

I smile weakly. It's been a long night and I'm still terrified for Eli.

"The last temperature check was going down," I tell Derek. "They're still waiting on the test results."

Derek nods slowly, rubbing at his arms.

"Thank you for being here, Kenna," he says softly.

I frown at him. "Where else would I be?"

He shakes his head. "You didn't have to be here," he says, and I feel a little offended. Does he really think I wouldn't come when one of the kids is sick?

"I know that you don't think very highly of me," I say softly. "But I love these kids, Derek. Just like they're my own."

I subconsciously rub my stomach and then catch myself, putting my hand back around Maggie. Derek doesn't seem to notice.

"I know you do," he says finally, and I look over at him. "I fucked this up, didn't I?" he asks with a half-smile.

"Royally," I say dryly, but then he chuckles and my heart breaks a little bit more. "But none of that matters. All that matters right now is that Eli's okay."

Derek nods. "I'll go back to stay with him if you'll take a shift with Maggie. I'll call my Mom so that you can get a break."

"I'm not leaving," I say firmly, and Derek smiles.

"I didn't think you would, but I wanted to give you the option."

I watch him walk back through the double doors, and I'm just dozing off again when Maggie wakes up, rubbing her eyes.

"Kenna? Where are we?"

I take in a deep breath. It's going to be a long night.

27

DEREK

The only thing keeping me going by morning is hospital coffee and Kenna Lodge. She's been a godsend during this awful time, and she's occupying Maggie so that I can spend as much time with Eli as I can.

Eli still calls for Kenna, still calling her "mama," and I can't bring myself to correct him. My kids love Kenna, and I'm starting to understand that I do, too, no matter how much I've tried to lie to myself.

Do I know what to do about it?

Absolutely not.

For now, all I can think about is getting Eli better.

When the doctor comes out to talk to me, it's one of the rare times that I've come out to check on Maggie, and so Kenna's with me. Maggie's asleep in one of the other chairs.

She takes my hand as the doctor explains that Eli has viral meningitis, not bacterial, and so we need to quarantine from him.

"So, he's going to be okay?" I ask, squeezing Kenna's hand too hard.

The doctor nods. "In about a week. For now, we'd like to keep him in the hospital for a few days to make sure he responds to medication for his symptoms."

I let out a long sigh of relief. "Thank you, doctor," I say, and hug Kenna tightly. I told Kenna that I would call my mother, but I haven't, not yet. I was too worried that something terrible would be wrong, and we were handling things.

Kenna hugs me back and excuses herself to the bathroom.

When I turn back to the waiting area, Maggie's awake and staring at me with big hazel eyes.

"Daddy?" she calls.

"What's up, sweetie?"

"Is Eli okay?"

"He's sick and you can't see him for a few days so that you won't get sick too, but he's going to be okay," I assure her.

"Hmm," Maggie hums. "And are you going to marry Kenna?"

I freeze. "What?"

"Are you going to marry Kenna? Is she gonna be our mommy?"

"Maggie," I start, but she keeps talking.

"Eli would really like that," she says firmly, and then looks away. "Maybe I'd like it, too."

"You would?" I ask softly, but Kenna's back and Maggie occupies herself with her coloring book as if nothing happened at all.

I look up at Kenna when she arrives and she smiles softly.

"What?" she asks.

I shake my head, my cheeks burning as I look away. "Nothing."

It's not like Kenna would forgive me. It's not like I deserve her. I'm still not worthy of her, and nothing is going to change that. But for a second, I wonder, what if...

It feels awkward sitting there without speaking much to Kenna, but at the same time, there's not much I can talk to her about with Maggie right here.

I clear my throat after a few minutes. "I'll be back. Going to call my mother," I mumble, and head out into the hallway.

My mother answers on the second ring. It's very early in the morning and I've already called into work.

"What's wrong?"

I never call her this early, so of course she's worried.

"It's Eli," I tell her, and explain his diagnosis.

"Oh, no," she breathes. "I'll be there as soon as I can."

"It's okay, Mom," I tell her easily. "Kenna's here with me."

She pauses on the other line. "That's your nanny? She's at the hospital with you?"

"Yeah?" I say, somewhat defensively.

"That's kind of going above and beyond, isn't it?"

"She's very good with the kids," I say tightly.

"Hmm."

I sigh. "Mom, what does that mean?"

"What does what mean?"

"That sound."

"Hmm?"

"Yes, that one," I say, exasperated.

"It's nothing, Derek. Focus on Eli."

I huff out a breath, frustrated. My mother has something to say, and she won't say it.

"Not until you tell me what you mean."

"They're getting really close to her, aren't they? They talked about her all weekend."

"Is that a bad thing?" I ask.

"I don't know," my mother says. "It might be, if she's just an employee."

"Of course she's just an employee," I mutter, although I'm lying to her and probably to myself. Kenna is much more than an employee, and she has been for quite some time.

"I trust you know what you're doing, son. Tell Eli Nana loves him."

I hang up with a deep sigh and turn back to the waiting area, where Kenna and Maggie are coloring together. She's always so engaged with them, and it's taught me to be more engaged with them too. So many things changed just from meeting Kenna, and I don't know how to make things right.

I've already ruined things with her this past weekend, but I don't want to ruin it for my kids.

"I'll take a turn with Maggie," I say, and Kenna gets up a little stiffly. I frown after her, but I'm not sure what's going on with her.

"I'll grab some lunch for us," I say, and Kenna nods, looking a little pale. I know she has to be hungry and exhausted, and part of me wants to tell her to go home and get some rest, but I know that she won't leave Eli.

She heads back to be with Eli and I take Maggie to the car.

"Are you *sure* you're not going to marry Kenna?" she asks, and I groan.

"Kenna's your nanny, Maggie."

"So?"

"So, I can't marry your nanny," I tell her as I'm buckling her into her seat.

"Why not?" she asks, pouting.

"Because," I say finally, and thank god, Maggie lets it go.

I've called in for the whole week at work, and I've gotten texts from both Grayson and Loxton asking how Eli is, so I answer them while I'm waiting at the drive-thru.

I return to the hospital with Maggie in tow and burgers in my hand, and when I arrive, Kenna isn't in the waiting room. I frown and check with the nurse.

"Could you go and get my....nanny," I say finally, not sure what to call her, "from the back?"

"Eli Ledderman?" she asks, and I nod.

The nurse disappears and finally, Kenna comes out of Eli's room, bracing her hand on the wall next to her.

"Come and sit down," I order, putting the burger in her hands, and Kenna smiles weakly.

"Thanks. I think I've just been awake too long," she says, and I frown at her.

"You should go home and get some rest," I suggest, and expect her to shake her head, but she doesn't, just looking down at her burger. "Kenna?"

She blinks, looking up at me. "Maybe I should," she mumbles.

"You're too tired to drive," I tell her. "I'll call you a car."

She looks almost green looking at the burger, but I make her eat at least a few fries, and soon enough, there's color back in her cheeks.

I call the car and steady her as she stands unsteadily.

"Kenna, are you all right?" I ask, and her smile this time is a little stronger.

"You need to sleep, Kenna," Maggie says, ushering her outside to the car as I smile at my independent daughter.

"I will, promise," Kenna says, waving at us as she gets into the backseat of the car.

I know after a good nap, she'll feel a lot better.

My mother shows up and takes a turn with Maggie so that I can go back to see Eli.

"Where's Mama?" he asks, and I wince, knowing that I'll have to have a conversation with him when he's better.

"Kenna's taking a nap," I say, sitting on the chair near the bed. They have a bubble around his bed now that they have the meningitis diagnosis. He needs to be quarantined and it sucks that I can't be closer to him. "Maggie drew you some train pictures." I show him her coloring book through the sheer plastic.

"Oh, wow," he says, seeming a little disappointed that Kenna isn't there but interested in his sister's drawings.

I watch him for a bit, as he drifts off, wondering what the hell I'm going to do about how attached he and Maggie are to Kenna. The best thing to do in this situation would be to part ways, so that I'm not tempted to talk to her, to kiss her, to be with her.

If I can't give her my heart, and I know I can't because I don't have one to give anymore, or I would, I have to stop playing with her emotions. I need to let her go, as hard as that is for me. I don't want to think about Kenna not being here for me and the kids. I especially don't want to think about her meeting someone else, having her second sexual partner.

It makes my skin crawl.

But I have to make a choice. And giving her my heart is not really a choice, so I have to push her away...for good.

I just don't know how I'll break it to my kids.

28

———

KENNA

I feel awful, but I guess that's what happens when you're pregnant and you stay up for the better part of two days without much food. I know I have to take better care of myself now that I'm carrying Derek's baby, but I just couldn't leave Eli until he felt a little better.

Luckily, I have the whole house to myself and I can just relax. I make it back home and fall down on the couch immediately. I fall asleep within minutes, unable to keep my eyes open, but I don't sleep for very long.

I wake up with a splitting headache and my neck is a bit stiff from the bad position I was sleeping in. I stumble to the kitchen to get some water. It helps a bit, and I decide to get to my room. There seems to be a lot of stairs and it takes me a lot longer than usual to get there, my head killing me with each step. I should probably call my doctor, but for now, I just need to get some rest.

I black out as soon as my head touches the pillow.

I wake up to a slight knock on my open door and bolt upright, wincing and holding my head.

"Shit," Derek curses. "I'm sorry. I didn't mean to wake you so violently. Everything's okay. My mom is staying with Eli so I can get some rest. Maggie's in her room."

"What time is it?" I ask, squinting at my phone.

"It's a little after six."

"In the *morning*?" I ask, shocked.

Derek smiles. "You must have been tired. You can go back to sleep, I just wanted to let you know we're home for today."

He looks exhausted, bags under his eyes, and I know how tired he must be, too. My headache apparently has come to stay for a while, and I don't know what's wrong with me.

Is pregnancy usually this awful?

It's not like I have anything to compare it to, or anyone to ask. Other than Cherie, no one knows I'm pregnant. And I could ask Derek, but Eli is still at the hospital and he needs his rest so he can be there for the little guy, so I don't want to add to his burden, right now. I'll just rest some more and maybe this will go away soon. If not, when Eli is better, if Derek is talking to me, I can tell him then and then I can ask how normal this is.

For now, it's a good thing I thought to put away the ultrasound pictures that were scattered on the bed.

Derek just keeps standing there, looking down at me.

"Are you okay?" I ask gently, and he nods slowly.

"I miss you in my bed," he says, and then blushes, looking away. "I'm sorry. That came out wrong. I didn't mean sexually," he stutters out. "I mean, I just miss holding you."

"You don't have to miss me," I say, my heart thudding hard against my chest plate.

"Not tonight?" he asks, and I know what he means. I know he doesn't mean forever, but I've been so worried about Eli and Derek, too, and maybe I'll take whatever I can get.

It might sound desperate, but I've never been in love before. I don't know how to deal with it.

Derek holds out his hand and I stand up, taking it and letting him lead me to his bedroom. I've showered and put on a pair of yoga shorts and a tank top, and Derek's hand slides along my stomach when I climb into bed with him.

My heart stutters in my chest as he slides his fingers around me, holding me tight. I wish I could tell him about the baby. I wish he could have his hand there because he knows, because he's excited about the new life we're bringing into the world.

But for now, he needs to focus on Eli and on him getting better. I can't be selfish and have him focus on me or this baby yet. In a week, Eli will be better and Derek's head will be in a better place and then I'll tell him. If he'll listen to me.

It takes me a long time to fall asleep, thinking of all the scenarios that may unfold when we talk about this baby, and when I finally drift off to sleep, I know Derek will be gone by the time I open my eyes again.

It's nearing dusk by the time I wake, and Derek's still wrapped around me tightly, his erection pressing up against my back. I swallow hard. This isn't the first time, after this weekend, but it still feels new somehow because of everything that's happened.

I pull away and Derek whines in the back of his throat, grabbing me around the waist and pulling me closer. Then he rolls his hips against my ass, making me catch my breath in my throat.

"Derek," I say softly. "Are you still sleeping?"

"Not anymore," he mumbles, kissing along my shoulder.

God, I know I shouldn't give in. He all but told me that he's not interested in me. He repeatedly pushed me away for being too young.

But it feels so good, and I want him so bad. I want him to love me, but I also want his touch, his lovemaking. Derek yanks my shorts down, palming across my ass before he rolls his hips up against me again.

"Should we be doing this?" I ask, and Derek pauses.

"Probably not," he admits, but he keeps rolling his hips, keeps kissing along my shoulder and my neck, and finally he pushes my shorts off, lifting one of my legs as he slides into me.

I clamp my hand over my mouth, knowing that Maggie might hear me, and my moan is muffled against my palm.

"Fuck, you feel so good," Derek whispers close to my ear, rocking up into me lazily, almost sleepily.

His hands reach around to cup my breasts, his thumbs skating across the peaks as I pant.

"Kenna," he moans against my ear, and my name on his lips sounds like music to my ears.

"Tell me you want me," I demand, dropping my hand from my mouth.

"I always want you," Derek responds easily, squeezing my breasts in his hands.

I groan, coming easily with the way he's angling up inside me, and Derek lets out a string of hushed curses, following me after just a few more thrusts.

He's always more worked up in the mornings, I found out this weekend.

The pitter patter of little feet sound in the hallway and Derek quickly pulls out of me.

I get out of Derek's bed immediately and run to the bathroom, hiding in there.

Derek yawns and shifts, and I hear Maggie ask about Eli while I'm standing in the bathroom, looking at myself in the mirror.

What am I even doing? Giving in to Derek like I did? Sleeping in his bed?

Hiding in the place I've called home for the last few months? And why? Because Derek doesn't think I'm good enough. I swallow hard. He doesn't think I'm good enough to be with him publicly, even if I'm good enough to bring into his bed in the still of the night away from prying eyes. But I deserve to be more than a dirty little secret, don't I? I deserve to be loved.

Eli getting sick made me forget for a while, but I know what I have to do. As soon as Eli is better and home, I'm going to quit this job.

No matter how much it might break my heart.

When I hear Derek leave the room with Maggie, I sneak back to my room, climbing back in the bed and pulling the covers over my head.

The next thing I know, Maggie is taking a flying leap into my bed and my headache jumps back to the front of my head. I wince but Maggie doesn't seem to notice.

"Kenna, Eli's getting out of the hospital!" she cheers.

"That's wonderful, Maggie," I tell her, and her hazel eyes are bright and she hugs me tightly. I can't help but smile, hugging her back even with the pain in my head.

Derek comes to the door next. "We're going to pick him up, now." He frowns, looking at me in the bed.

"Maybe you should get some more rest."

I shake my head, sitting up on the edge of the bed. "I want to be with him when he's released," I say, biting my lip.

I want to see Eli because after he's home, I'm going to be moving out.

I ride quietly with Derek and Maggie as she chatters in the backseat. I look out the window, my head pounding. I guess I haven't gotten enough rest or maybe I haven't eaten enough. After all, I haven't had a real meal except for a few fries in a while.

I wait in the lobby with Maggie, sitting down so that my knees don't feel weak, while Derek goes to the back to get Eli.

My vision seems to be blacking in and out, and I'm getting a bit worried when Derek carries Eli out.

"Mama," Eli says happily, and throws himself into my arms.

I look up at Derek, but he's just smiling down at Eli, seemingly unbothered by what Eli's calling me. It breaks my heart to think about leaving him and Maggie, but I don't know what else to do. How else to resist the man that doesn't think I good enough or old enough to want to be with me.

I can't just be near Derek and the kids and keep loving them more and more each day and wanting what I can't have. I'll tell him about the baby as soon as I move out. I don't want him to feel compelled to offer me room and board just because I'm expecting his baby.

I want nothing from him except what I now know he'll never be able to give me. His heart. We'll coparent, of course, but I can't be in that house every day and not be part of the family. It just hurts too much.

My arms go around Eli and squeeze him as tight as I can, but I'm too weak to squeeze hard.

"Eli," I try to say, but my words seem slurred, and Derek frowns.

"Kenna?" he calls, but it sounds like his voice is coming from far away. I try to stand up and hand Eli back to him, but my knees buckle, and all I can hope is that Derek is able to grab Eli as my knees buckle and I black out.

29

DEREK

Eli screams as Kenna falls to the floor and I catch him, and I quickly put him down next to his sister, calling for a nurse, a doctor, anyone.

Kenna's crumpled on the floor and I crouch down on the ground, scooping her up into my lap and touching her face. My heart is in my throat and I can't think; I can only react.

"Kenna?" I ask, shocked. "Kenna, don't do this."

My voice breaks when I call out for a doctor again, and Eli and Maggie are both crying.

When finally a male nurse comes with a stretcher to take her back, I stand up, all nervous energy.

"What's wrong with her?" I ask. "She fainted, she just won't wake up."

The nurse looks at me. "Is this your wife?" he asks.

"She's our nanny," Maggie sobs, and I curse under my breath. I would have lied, honestly, would have said she's my wife to get some information, to get back there with her, but now they whisk her away and I crouch with Maggie and Eli, trying to comfort them.

Eli's crying out "mama, mama, mama" over and over and

I don't know how to make him feel better. I don't know how to make *myself* feel better. It occurs to me suddenly that Kenna has spent just as much time with Eli as I have, and my blood goes cold.

What if she's caught his meningitis?

It's very survivable if it's viral, so she'll be okay, surely, but I can't stop thinking the worst. There are cases when people die from meningitis, right? Or have something like brain damage? Hell, that's what I've been worried about with Eli, so it's certainly possible that she could have it, too. What am I going to do?

I'm not related to her and I have no idea how to contact her parents. I try three different times to get information from a nurse or a doctor, but I'm shot down each time.

I feel shell-shocked, barely able to think, but then I see Kenna's bag in the chair she's vacated and I dig through it, finding her cell phone.

Calling her mother is a strange thing for me to do, especially since my children are still quietly sobbing after watching her pass out.

"Ms. Lodge?" I ask, and she makes a noise in the back of her throat.

"Yes?"

"Ah, I'm Derek Ledderman, we've met?"

"Oh! Derek, yes, of course!"

"Kenna and I are at the hospital. She fainted. I don't know what's wrong and they won't tell me anything..."

"Oh, god," she gasps. "Which hospital? I'll be there as soon as I can."

"Vincent Presbyterian," I say, relieved.

I'm oddly nervous to meet Kenna's parents, and they end up bringing the whole family, including her brother and sister. Maggie immediately takes a shine to the sister, Kimberly, even though she's twice her age.

"What happened?" Frank, Kenna's father asks me, and I've met him a few times before because of course, he's Suzanna's brother.

"She just fainted out of nowhere," I say, but then pause. " That's not true. She hasn't been sleeping, or eating really, because Eli's been sick with meningitis..."

"Meningitis," Frank gasps, and I bite my lip.

I've handled this poorly. I should have paid more attention to what Kenna was eating, how she was sleeping. I was just so worried about Eli that I couldn't see anything else.

When Kenna's mother returns from the back, her face is pale. "They won't tell me much, either, but they say they're testing her for meningitis."

"Shit," I curse.

"When can we see her?" Frank asks, and his wife shakes her head.

"I don't know."

She looks over at me. "Thank you so much for calling, Derek. You can take the kids home now."

I stand there for a long moment, wanting to stay but not knowing how to explain why I want to stay.

I pick up Eli and Maggie, one on each hip, and start to leave, but that's when Eli loses it.

"We can't leave Mama!" he screams, and Maggie nods.

"We can't leave her," she says firmly, and I feel lost.

"You're welcome to stay," Frank says, and I slowly put the kids down, comforting Eli briefly as he leans against his sister, tired from the ordeal of being in the hospital and everything that happened earlier.

What am I going to do? Stuck here with my ex's family and my kids, not knowing whether Kenna is okay or not?

It's driving me crazy. I want to see her. I *need* to see her. I feel so helpless. I can't go home without her, especially with Eli so worried about her.

"How's Kenna been doing?" Frank asks, clearly nervous and needing to talk about something that isn't about how sick his daughter might be.

"She's amazing," I say honestly. "She's wonderful with the kids."

"She's always loved kids," he says softly. "Always wanted some of her own."

"She's so young," I marvel, but Frank laughs.

"Ken is an old soul. Always has been. She took on so much responsibility when she was young, taking care of her brother and sister."

I hum, not quite knowing what to say. Kenna *is* mature, after all, but she's so young to want kids. I hadn't even been near thinking about kids when I was a senior in college.

I leave the kids in their care for just a moment while I go to grab everyone some coffee, and when I return, the doctor is there, talking to Frank.

"She does have viral meningitis, but it's...a little more difficult with her situation," he says.

"What situation?" my mother asks.

The doctor flips through his paperwork. "I'm sorry, I'm not at liberty to do anything but give updates on her condition. Right now we're giving her IV antibiotics and she should rally. We just have to keep an eye on her."

Her situation? What is that supposed to mean? Has Kenna been sick?

"When can we see her?" Frank asks.

"In a few hours, when she's gotten some rest," the doctor says. "She's suffering from exhaustion on top of the fever, and we need her more stable before visitors."

Frank slumps slightly and I clear my throat, handing out coffees.

"Thank you," Kenna's mother says, and I'm wishing that I could remember her name. It's been years since I've met her, and I feel slightly guilty for not allowing the kids to know some of their cousins.

I guess when Suzanna left, I just wanted to get away from her entirely.

"We need to get home," I tell Maggie, because Eli has finally dropped off to sleep, and she pouts, looking up from the coloring book she's been showing Kimberly.

"We're leaving Kenna?"

Her words feel like little arrows in my heart, because I don't want to leave, either. I want to see her, to make sure she's okay, but her family is here and they deserve to see her. Also, I can't explain that I'm in love with their daughter, which is why I'm so invested.

"We'll come back when she can have visitors," I promise.

I pick up Eli gingerly as to not wake him, and Maggie follows behind, holding my hand.

We make it back home and the kids are dead silent, clearly having been through a hard few days.

Eli is stuck to me like glue and both kids end up in my bed that night, asking about Kenna (or in Eli's case, Mama) and when she'll be back.

I can't believe I ever thought that I could ask Kenna to stop working for me. I cannot rip her away from my kids the way that their mother was ripped away.

I have a lot of thinking to do. I have to figure out what I want, between my heart and my brain, and make a real decision.

30

KENNA

When I come to, I'm inside a plastic bubble and my mother is standing over my bed, staring down at me. "McKenna Anne Lodge," she gasps. "You scared me to death."

I blink at her, feeling groggy and realizing that my arm has an IV in it.

"What happened?" I ask, still feeling out of it.

"You fainted because you haven't been taking care of yourself," she scolds. "The doctor says you got meningitis because your immune system is low."

I swallow hard. "Mom—" I start, scrambling to sit up. "I need to speak to the doctor."

She freezes. "What's wrong? Are you not feeling well?"

"I just need to speak to the doctor. Right now," I say harshly, worried about the baby. They don't know that I'm pregnant, and they need to check out the baby.

"Okay, okay," my mother says, frowning, and walks out to the nurse's station to get a nurse.

"Mom, I need the room," I say, and my mother glares at

me. "Please," I say, my voice cracking, and my mother, who has always trusted me, she trusts me now, leaving the room.

"I'm ten weeks pregnant," I croak out, and the nurse reassures me they know and all seems fine, but now that I'm awake, she calls in another nurse for a fetal heartbeat monitor.

My heart beats way too wildly but the baby's heartbeat is strong and normal. I sigh in relief, fighting back tears.

"Do you want me to call your mother in?" the nurse asks gently, and I shake my head.

"No, thank you. I just want to rest."

I lie down and fall asleep so easily it surprises me when I wake up hours later with a nurse knocking on my door.

She asks if I want to see a visitor and I say yes, thinking it will be my mother. Thinking fast, I throw a blanket over the fetal monitor screen.

Instead of my mother, it's my father, and he looks pale.

"Hey, Ken," he says softly, and I can't help it, I burst into tears.

"Daddy," I tell him, unable to keep it in anymore. "Oh Daddy, I'm sorry. But..."

My sobs take the best of me. My dad's eyes widen in panic.

"What is it, honey? Should I go and get someone? A doctor? Your mother?"

I'm trying to shake my head frantically, but it hurts. "No, Daddy, it's just that...I...I'm pregnant." And my sobs intensify.

My father blinks rapidly. "Wh-what?"

"I'm going to have a baby," I say, when I calm down a bit, looking away from him, not wanting to see the look of disappointment on his face.

When I look up at him, though, it isn't disappointment but concern I see in his expression.

"The father..." he starts, and I shake my head.

"Can we not talk about him for now? Please?"

I can't tell him that his ex-brother-in-law, his sister, my aunt's ex-husband, who is also my employer, is the father of my baby. Not when I haven't even told Derek yet. He deserves to know that from me.

My father swallows. "Whatever you want, Ken."

I grab the blanket and remove it from the fetal heartbeat monitor, showing him the strong and steady heartbeat.

"Oh my god," my father breathes, and sits down hard on the chair by my bed.

"Dad, I'm sorry," I begin, but he cuts me off.

"You want this baby?" he asked, looking right at me.

"Yes," I say confidently. "I've always wanted kids, and even though this isn't how I imagined it...." I trail off, not knowing how to explain it.

He takes in a deep breath and lets it out slowly.

"I can't say I'm happy about how it happened, since I didn't even know you were seeing someone, but I'm excited to be a grandfather," he says in a low voice, and I can't stop crying.

I've always been such a good girl, always taken care of everyone, and it feels nice to have my father taking care of me.

"Will you tell Mom for me?" I ask hesitantly, and my father nods.

"I wish I could hug you right now, baby."

"Me too, Daddy," I say as a few stray tears slide down my cheeks.

He walks outside for a few moments and then my mother comes running back into the room.

"I should have known," she insists. "I knew something was going on with you."

"It's okay, Mom," I assure her, holding my hand to the bubble as she does the same on the other side, as we both crave each other's touch even if through sheer plastic. "I'm okay. The baby's okay."

"You have to take better care of yourself and that grand-baby of mine."

I smile weakly. "I will, Mom. Promise."

"I don't know who this father is, but if he is out of the picture, we don't need him," she insists. "We will help you raise this baby. He's ours just as much as he is yours, right?"

I can't tell them who it is, it wouldn't be fair to Derek that they found out before him, but hearing my mom, I wipe tears from my eyes, grateful that they're being so supportive.

"Thank you so much, Mom," I say tiredly. "The dad doesn't know yet, so I have no idea how he'll react. But it's good knowing that regardless of his reaction, I can count on you guys."

"Always, baby. Now, you need to get your rest," she says, and I nod slowly.

"I do," I admit.

She blows me a kiss and walks out the door, and I'm left alone with my own thoughts.

Luckily, I'm not trapped in my own head for long. The doctor comes in with an ultrasound machine, and I get to see for myself the little peanut that's inside my belly is nice and healthy. I keep thinking about the future, about how I don't know if I'll be with Derek and have the family that I want, and I start crying and can't stop. It's all too much.

"Please, calm down, Ms. Lodge," the doctor says gently. "You need to not stress yourself so much, or you might lose this pregnancy."

I gasp. "Due to stress?"

"Stress and the meningitis are both dangerous for the fetus," she explains. "So, you need to take it easy. I recommend bed rest until you're free from the meningitis, so I'd like to keep you in the hospital for another few days."

I nod slowly. "Of course," I say, wiping at my eyes.

I seem to have sprung a leak and I can't plug it up. I guess it's the hormones, plus all the stress I've been under with everything happening with Derek and taking care of a sick Eli and this little guy inside my belly.

I wonder briefly how Eli's doing, feeling a pang in my heart thinking about the young boy. I want him and Maggie to be well, and I wish I knew what's going on with them. I can't very well expect Derek to visit me in the hospital – for all intents and purposes, I'm just his employee, after all.

When the doctor leaves, I sigh, rubbing my stomach. I miss the kids, and I miss Derek, and I wish that I could share this with him from the start.

But if he doesn't even want to face me or talk to me, how am I supposed to tell him about this baby? I can't just force him to listen, can I? Now that Eli is okay again, I could tell him, but I'm not sure I'm strong enough while I'm here to handle the rejection. Except, am I not in the right place to mend a broken heart if it comes to that?

I need to stop worrying about this, especially since I'm almost sure I'll only see him when I go to the house. For now, I'm under doctor's orders to sleep and rest plenty, so I close my eyes and eventually drift off.

When I wake up, I feel disoriented, thinking I'm back in my room at Derek's mansion. When I realize where I am, I feel disappointed, but at the same time, I guess I'm glad I don't have to deal with his cold shoulder for a few days at least.

There's a knock on the door, and instinctively, I throw the blanket over the fetal monitor again, even though my parents already know. It turns out it's good that I did, because Derek Ledderman walks in the door.

31

DEREK

When I walk into the hospital hallway, Frank is talking about a baby. I don't think much of it, and when I walk into Kenna's hospital room, she looks a little pale.

"How are you doing?" I ask, putting the vase of flowers down on the side table.

"Oh, Derek, they're beautiful," she murmurs, looking at the arrangement from inside the plastic bubble. "I'm doing a lot better, thank you."

Her voice sounds flat but she must be tired, so I don't pry.

"I wanted to say how sorry I am that Eli got you sick," I say, sitting down awkwardly on the chair across from the bed.

I don't know how to say that she's changed my life and the kid's life too. I don't know how to say I'm afraid that I'm falling in love with her just as my kids have fallen in love with her, so instead, I just say that I'm sorry.

I'm sorry for more than Eli getting her sick, but I don't say that, either.

"It's not his fault," Kenna says, frowning. "How's he doing? Has Maggie gotten sick?"

I shake my head. "Luckily, no. The doctors say he's not contagious anymore, and he's been fine, just a little lethargic as he's getting better."

Kenna lets out a breath of relief. "Thank God," she says. "I worry about him and Maggie all the time."

"I know you do," I say warmly. "I wanted to thank you, Kenna, for all you've done for my family."

She frowns again. "Why does this sound like you're firing me?"

"Oh, god, no," I say quickly. "I couldn't fire you if I wanted to. My kids would mutiny," I joke, trying to keep it light, but Kenna's brows are still drawn together. "Don't worry. Your job isn't going anywhere."

"I think we maybe should start cutting down my hours," she says quietly. "I'll be going back to school, soon."

The idea of her leaving and going back to college makes my heart seize up, but I would never hold her back. She's going to college out of state, so cutting her hours means she'll soon quit all together. I guess I always knew this would be temporary, but it still guts me.

I swallow hard. "We'll figure it out," I say, looking at her curiously. "You look so tired, sweetheart. Should I leave so that you can rest?"

Kenna shakes her head. "No. All I've been doing is sleeping," she complains. "I want to hear more about the kids. I miss them."

"They miss you, too," I assure her, and they do. And so do I, but I don't tell her that. "They want to visit but I don't want to risk them getting sick."

"Of course not," she says. "Maybe I'll call them tonight."

I smile. "That would be nice. They'd love to hear your voice."

"Derek," she starts, and then pauses. She takes a sip of water and then starts again. "About Eli calling me Mama—"

I cut her off. "It happens, right?"

"Has it happened before?" she asks.

I shake my head slowly. "No, but it just means that he's attached to you. We knew that was going to happen."

"I think that's another reason why I need to cut my hours," she says, and my heart aches again. I know there are other reasons she wants to cut back on her hours, and it's my fault.

She is doing what I wanted all along, pulling away. Last week, hell, yesterday, I would have gladly said yes, so why does it destroy me to hear her talking about stepping back? Leaving us.

"About us, Kenna," I try to begin, but she holds up her hand.

"I know how you feel about that," she says, although she doesn't. I've only figured out how I feel about it recently, but I don't contradict her. "We don't have to talk about it."

I keep quiet, not sure what to say next.

"Is there anything you need?" I ask. "Something to eat?"

She shakes her head, and I realize it's a little gingerly, like her neck is stiff. It's a symptom I've noticed with Eli.

"I can't keep much down," she admits. "But if you'd be so kind as to bring some of my books from home..."

"Of course," I say easily. "Write me a list and I'll bring whatever you need."

"Where are the kids?" she asks.

"With my mother," I say with a sigh. "She's been helping me out a lot since Eli got sick."

Kenna swallows. "Maybe you don't need me as much as you think you do."

I look up into her blue eyes. "That's not true," I say quietly. "We need you at home, Kenna."

"At least until I go back to school," she says.

I look away. "At least until then."

"You didn't have to come," she says almost irritably, looking right at me.

I lift my head to look at her again. "You don't want me to visit?"

Kenna bites her lip. "I didn't say that."

I chuckle low in my throat. "You're contradicting yourself, sweetheart."

"Don't call me that," she says softly. "Not if you don't mean it."

Her blue eyes are watery.

"What if I do mean it?" I ask in a mumble under my breath, and Kenna blinks at me.

"What did you say?"

I shake my head. "Nothing," I say, my heart beating too hard. I can't tell her now how I feel about her. This is not the time or the place. She is in the hospital, inside a plastic bubble and I can't even touch her. And there's too much baggage between us. Besides, Kenna deserves someone younger and less jaded. But I am selfish. I want her with me. I want to tell her that I'm falling for her, that my kids love her as a mom, that I want us to give this thing a try and to hell with what is right or wrong with our age gap. But I want to show it to her too. I want to hold her in my arms while I show her with my kiss, with my touch, that she is it for me.

I can wait until she leaves the hospital, until she's better so she can focus on recovering, but I can't let her go without letting her know the impact she's made in our lives. *My* life.

Thinking about her gone guts me. The thought of her with some kid her own age makes my body fill with anger. But I want her to be happy, so I'll do whatever she needs me to do. Even if that means letting her go forever.

And unless I tell her how I feel, that's what's going to happen, when she goes back to college. Even if I tell her, I have no guarantee she won't leave us, but I'm willing to take that chance now.

As soon as she is back home, I'll tell her, and we can go from there. For now, she just needs to get better.

Kenna writes me a list of things she needs from home and I take it from her.

"Get some rest," I say quietly, and she nods in that stiff way she has now.

I sigh heavily as I walk out of the room and into the lobby, running my hand through my hair.

Kenna's going back to college. She's leaving us, and I'll miss her. I'll miss her so terribly I don't know how I'll deal with it.

After I rejected her so harshly, I need to tell her the truth. I need her to know how I really feel. I just can't tell her that here.

When I get back home, my mother looks frazzled.

"How is she doing?" she asks immediately.

"She's okay," I say, hugging her. "How was Eli?"

"Eli was fine," she says flatly. "It's Maggie who was a little gremlin."

I laugh, unable to help it. "She's acting out because Eli is getting all the attention?"

"She keeps saying Kenna does this and that differently," my mother huffs. "She loves that nanny of yours."

She's not the only one, I think but don't say.

"She'll be back for a bit before she goes back to school."

My mother stares at me for a moment. "Don't you think you need to talk to the kids about how she won't be around all the time? They're getting really attached."

I swallow hard. I haven't thought about that, but she's right. If she still chooses to leave, even if it's not forever, the kids should have a heads up. And if she chooses to go forever... I can't even think about the possibility right now.

"I'll talk to them," I assure her.

I have no idea what I'll say, and so I don't do it that night. My mother leaves and I bathe the kids and get them in bed, and they go to sleep fairly easily.

Even Maggie seems tired after driving her grandmother crazy all day, and they both ask me about Kenna, although Eli's still calling her Mama.

"She's going to be okay," I tell Maggie, and she frowns a little.

"But she's still in the hospital."

"Yes, she's getting better there. Just like Eli."

"She's been in the hospital *forever*," she complains.

I chuckle. "It's only been a couple of days."

"But she has to stay longer and can't come home," she argues sleepily, burrowing under the covers.

I kiss her cheek. "She'll be out before you know it," I say, not mentioning that she'll only be around half the time.

I don't know how to talk to the kids about Kenna leaving, because I don't know how to deal with it myself.

32

———

KENNA

I have no idea how to tell Derek that I'll be going back to school sooner rather than originally planned. In fact, I'm thinking about moving back as soon as I get out of the hospital. The thought of being around him all day every day and him just going back to his old self, ignoring me, and dismissing me because of my age hurts too much. And this "sweetheart" thing? What the hell was that? Is he treating me like a child?

And speaking of child. I need to tell him, sooner rather than later. I'll be showing soon. But maybe I'll wait until after I move out so that there is less stress for the baby and me. I already know he doesn't want me because of my age, so if I'm living there when I tell him, he'll find some excuse to get me to stay or he'll think he has to do 'the right thing'. I don't want him to think he needs to be with me just because we're having a baby.

The point is I *have* to leave. Leave him. Leave the kids. I can't imagine leaving Eli and Maggie without breaking down, so I try not to think about it.

Derek comes to visit every day, bringing me new books,

193

flowers, and stuffed animals. I don't know why he's doing all this. Why he is always here. He wasn't even looking at me when Eli got sick. Does he feel guilty thinking this is his fault because I caught Eli's meningitis?

Even my parents think he's going overboard, and tease me about how I must be a phenomenal nanny, and I just smile weakly.

Derek returns today with a box with all my things I've written down for him to get, and I thank him profusely.

"It's no problem," he insists, rubbing the back of his neck. "There's also a couple of presents in there from Eli and Maggie."

I'm no longer contagious, so the bubble is gone, but the doctor asked me to stay in the hospital a couple days more to see if all is well with the baby. I look through the box and there's drawings from Eli and a couple of notes from Maggie. Maggie writes about how she's been playing unicorns with her grandmother but it's not the same. She says she wants me to come home soon.

I can't help breaking into tears, and Derek takes a few hesitant steps toward me.

"Kenna?" he asks. "What's wrong?"

"I'll just miss them so much," I sob.

"What do you mean? You'll get to see them soon enough," he says, trying to comfort me.

I shake my head. "I won't see them for long," I mutter. "I need to get moved back as soon as possible."

Derek's face goes pale. "Kenna, how far away is your college?"

"It's in Washington," I say softly, and Derek sets his jaw.

"You're going back to college *hours* away?"

I stare at him. Doesn't he understand that if he can't love

me, I can't be anywhere close by? But I can't tell him that. "It's my career, Derek."

"You're already doing your career," he argues. "This is what you wanted, right?"

"Yeah," I say, fighting tears. "This is what I wanted."

"I'm sorry," he says quietly, noticing the tears in my eyes. "I didn't mean to—"

"You didn't mean to what?" I can't help the tears streaming down my face.

Derek doesn't answer, and I realize that I'm too emotional. There's just too much going on in my head right now.

I sigh. "I'm sorry."

"You don't have to be sorry," he mumbles. "I fucked everything up, didn't I? And now you're leaving."

"Not right away," I say gently. "I'm going to talk to the kids first."

He nods slowly, still looking pale. "I'll talk to them, too."

"Do you think they'll be upset?"

He gives me a wry smile. "I think they'll be devastated."

I swallow hard. "I'm so sorry, Derek."

"I'm the one that's sorry," he says. "I ruined all of this by giving in to my baser instincts."

I wonder if Derek has any idea how much it hurts me that I was just a lapse in his judgment. I look away from him.

"We all make mistakes," I say. "Just give me a good reference, will you?"

"I'll give you a glowing recommendation," he assures me.

"Good," I mutter, and after a few awkward glances, he leaves.

My mother comes in right after and I'm breathing hard, fighting back tears.

"Honey, what's wrong?"

"I don't know," I say miserably, even though I do. It's like I've found this little family that I so desperately want to be a part of, and I'm being forced out.

She chuckles. "I remember being hormonal with you. The first baby is always the hardest."

"Yeah?" I asked, wiping at my eyes irritably. "I feel like I'm crying all the time."

"I cried every day when I was pregnant with you," my mother explained. "It's hard, being pregnant. You've got all these emotions on top of the hormones."

I nod slowly.

"Everything's going to be okay, Kenna. We're going to help you, father or no father." She wrinkles her nose. "When you're all better, you're going to tell me about him."

I smile weakly. "Okay, Mom." That would at least give me time to cultivate a lie. There's no way I'm telling them that Derek Ledderman is my baby's father. I might tell him, because he has a right to know, but no one else needs to know whose this baby is but mine. Especially since I'll be moving so far away.

"Are you still planning on going back to school?"

"Yes," I say firmly. "I'll be able to go to classes up until my seventh month or so, and then I'll take some time off."

"You'll come home and let us take care of you?" she asks.

"I think I will," I admit, tired and emotional and taking the comfort she offers.

She hums and runs her hand through my hair. "We'll get through it, baby girl. We always do."

Tears threaten at the backs of my eyes again. "I know, Mom. Thank you."

"You've always been such a good girl," she muses. "I'm surprised it took you this long to rebel."

"I wasn't rebelling," I argue. "I'm a grown woman."

"It's hard to think of you that way," my mother says. "You'll see, when you have your baby."

"I guess I will," I muse, thinking of Maggie and how I would feel if she got pregnant as a young adult. I guess I would be worried, too.

Maggie and Eli feel like mine even though they're not, and I don't know how to reconcile that with having to part from them. I can't wait to see them, to hug them, to talk to them. It's going to be a hard conversation, but it has to be done.

The doctor comes in while my mother is comforting me, and she stands up to speak to her.

"Everything seems to be in order," the doctor says, "so I'm going to be discharging you today."

I smile widely, happy. "Thank goodness," I mumble.

"You'll come home with us?" my mother asks, and I shake my head.

"I need to see the kids," I say, and she frowns.

"I worry that you're getting too attached to them, Kenna."

"I guess I am," I mumble. "But I love those kids, Mom."

"I know you do," she soothes as the doctor walks out to get my discharge papers ready. "But you can't stress yourself out too much."

"I won't," I assure her, even though I'm not sure what I'm going to do. I guess I'll have to go home to Derek's and talk to the kids, spend maybe a week there to soak up some quality time with them.

By the time the doctor returns with the paperwork, my mother is ready to give me a ride home. I get dressed and take my little box of all my things that Derek brought me, including Maggie and Eli's drawings and get-well cards.

I show them to my mother and she smiles widely.

"We need to get back into their lives," she says softly. "Maybe Derek will let us see them while you're in college. They're your cousins, after all."

I nod slowly, thinking that it's strange to think of them as my cousins instead of my own children. I love them like they're my own.

My mother drives me to Derek's and marvels at how big the place is.

"Derek's done well for himself, hasn't he?" she comments, and I laugh.

"Yeah, slightly," I say. "I guess he's good at what he does."

I know that Derek is in marketing and sales, but his personality isn't anything like a salesman, so I wonder. I guess maybe he's different at work than he is around everyone else.

When I arrive at Derek's, Maggie's in the living room, which seems destroyed by toys, and Eli's lying on the couch.

Maggie turns to look at me and drops everything she's been holding, running toward me and jumping up into my arms.

I catch her with a groan and Derek comes walking in from the kitchen.

"Don't knock her over, she's still sick," he complains, and tries to take Maggie from me but she yells and I shake my head.

"She's fine," I say, taking her over to the couch so I can see Eli, too.

He leans against me and I put my hand in his hair.

"Being sick is no joke, huh?" I ask him, and he nods listlessly. I guess he isn't all better yet. I feel still tired and sore myself, especially in my neck area, so I can understand.

"We missed you *so* much, Kenna," Maggie says empathetically, hugging me tight around my neck.

"I missed you too, cupcake," I say, and she grins and buries her face in my neck.

"She's probably not feeling up to playing just yet," Derek warns, and Maggie frowns at him.

"I'm going to be gentle," she says, even though she's practically wringing my neck.

I smile at her, hugging her tight with one arm and putting an arm around Eli.

How did my aunt do this? Because they are not even really mine and I don't know how I'm *ever* going to leave them.

33

DEREK

As I sit there and watch Kenna with my kids, I can't understand the anger that's rising in me. I don't know why I feel so upset at the thought of her leaving, of her leaving the kids. Of her leaving *me*.

Feeling abandoned is the worst feeling in the world, but I know that Kenna leaving is my fault. I can't help all the old emotions that rise up in me, though, and I try to bite my tongue.

The kids are playing in the pool, Maggie dog-paddling in her floaties and Eli floating in his ring at the shallow end, when I pull Kenna aside.

"When are we going to tell them?" I ask her, and my voice is flat and cold.

"Soon," she responds under her breath, glancing back toward Eli and Maggie.

"We should do it sooner rather than later, since you're leaving," I snap, and Kenna narrows her eyes at me.

"I'm not leaving right away," she says softly.

I roll my shoulders around, feeling tense.

"I don't know how they'll take it," I say, but what I really mean is that I don't know how *I'll* take it.

"I don't either," she agrees. "But it has to be done."

It doesn't have to be done. You could stay here. Stay with me.

I clear my throat so I don't say what I'm thinking. I know I should talk to her, tell her the truth about how I feel, but I can't. I'm just so angry and love is not about anger. Besides, if she is really leaving, the kids needs to be able to have a proper goodbye and they need all the memories they can get.

"You're leaving them, just like their mother did," I say, not realizing that's what I was going to say, and Kenna gasps.

"I'm not leaving them," she said quietly but with anger just under the surface. "I'm leaving *you*. You're the one who gave up on this."

"Gave up on what?" I ask, and Kenna blinks again and I can see that her blue eyes have gone glassy and I hate myself.

"You know what," she hisses, and then Maggie calls for her and Kenna strips off her clothes, down to her bikini and I look away, not wanting to see the long line of her thighs or the curve of her back.

I don't want to be attracted to her right now. I want her just to be another employee, one who is leaving.

I stalk back into the house and grab myself a beer. I know she is right, It's all my fault. But I'm also afraid that even if I tell her the truth, even if I ask her to stay, she'll still leave. She'll still break my heart. Just like Suzanna did. But what if she doesn't? My heart leaps at that, as another voice in my head immediately counters, 'But what if she does?' and I deflate again.

It's going to be a long day.

I watch through the window of the kitchen as Kenna

swims with the kids, letting Maggie dunk her under the water.

They'll miss her so much.

I'll missed her so much.

I don't know how to do this. I don't know how to let her go, how not to feel abandoned all over again.

But Kenna isn't like Suzanna. I'm the one who ruined this.

After chugging my first beer, I grab another out of the fridge. It's Sunday, after all, and I don't go into work until the morning. Plus, Kenna's here to watch the kids and I need something to numb everything that I'm feeling right now.

By the time dinner rolls around, I'm clumsy after a six pack, making hamburgers and fries. I finally manage to get it done and Kenna frowns at me at the dinner table.

"What?" I ask her, and she gestures toward the beer bottles that I've deposited in the trash can.

I shrug. "It's my day off," I mutter, cracking open another one.

I don't usually act like this. I don't drink around the kids, but Kenna's back and all I can think about is that she's leaving.

The alcohol helps numb the abandonment and anger that I'm feeling, and I'm not going to stop just because Kenna disapproves.

She isn't my wife. She isn't their mother.

Even if part of me wishes that she was. A big part. Like all of me.

Eli throws a fit because he wants hot dogs instead of hamburgers but Kenna calms him down, putting his hamburger on a hot dog bun and adding ketchup and mustard.

I would have had no idea how to deal with a tantrum

like that, but she's perfect with the kids. She always has been.

I look at Eli and Maggie, the way they beam at her, how she can calm them down at a moment's notice, and I feel sick to my stomach, thinking that in a couple of weeks, she won't be here.

"Kenna's leaving," I burst out, trying to keep the slur out of my words, and Kenna glares at me.

"No, I'm not," she assures the kids.

"Never?" Eli asks, munching on his hamburger/hot dog.

"Not never," Maggie says matter-of-factly. "One day, she'll get married and have her own babies."

Kenna barks out a laugh that sounds a little bitter. "I don't know about that."

"Of course you will," I murmur, a dark feeling washing over me. "You'll meet some guy at college who will sweep you off your feet and be pregnant within a year."

Kenna stares at me, frowning. "Derek, what is wrong with you?" she hisses under her breath.

Maggie and Eli finish eating and run upstairs to play and Kenna grabs the dishes off the table. I take her wrist in my hand.

"You don't have to do that. Cecilia is coming tomorrow morning."

"It'll give her less work to do," Kenna snaps.

"Maggie's right, you know? Even if you weren't going to college, eventually, you'd leave them." I know I'm digging a hole I can't get out of, but despair has settled over me like a storm cloud.

"You're drunk," she accuses. "And you don't know what the hell you're talking about."

"Don't I? You're a beautiful young woman, Kenna."

"Is that so? Is that why you want nothing to do with me?"

"I'd lose you," I mutter, slumping down in my seat. "Lose you to some asshole college frat boy. You'd leave me."

"Shut *up*, Derek," Kenna says irritably. "You should go to bed."

I snort and look down at my watch. The numbers swirl around and I blink at it. "It's not even dark," I argue.

"Well, then you shouldn't have drank so much."

"I didn't drink that mu—" I look toward the trashcan and she's right, there's six bottles in there and one in my hand. I shrug. "It's Sunday," I defend myself.

"I'm glad you're enjoying yourself," she says, exasperated and loading the dishwasher, slamming it closed.

"Shouldn't I?" I shoot back. "It's one of the last weeks I'll have help."

"I don't know what you want from me, Derek," she sighs, walking back over toward the table to pick up my half a beer. I grab it from her and chug it defiantly before putting it back down on the table. Empty.

She scoffs and takes it, throwing it in the trash.

I sit there at the table, looking at her.

"I don't want you to go," I say finally, and there *is* a slur in my voice now and I know I should shut up, close my mouth right now.

"I know. You need help with the kids. You'll find someone else," she says easily.

"No," I say stubbornly. "Not that. I don't *want* you to go," I repeat, upset that I can't make her understand what I'm trying to say.

Kenna puts her hands on her hips, looking frustrated.

"So, you want me to stay?"

"Yes," I say, nodding my head eagerly but it makes me dizzy so I stop, looking at her. "I want you to stay."

"I need to finish college."

"Go to Berkeley," I suggest. "It's closer."

"All my credits are in Washington."

"They'll transfer," I insist, leaning forward and taking her hands in mine. "Stay here. Stay with the kids." I pause. "Stay with me."

"Why?" she asks in a soft voice, and my mouth goes dry, looking up at her.

"Because I need you," I murmur, pulling her closer, pressing my face into her stomach. Slowly, her hand goes into my hair, playing with the blond and gray strands.

"You'll find another nanny."

"I don't *want* another nanny," I insist, and Kenna sighs, pulling away from me.

"Let's get you to bed," she offers, and tugs my hand. I stand up unsteadily and follow her up the stairs, holding on to the railing.

She stops at my bedroom door but I pull her farther in, pulling her close and smelling the crown of her head. The room is spinning but I know I want her with me, don't want her to go.

"Stay," I say again. "Promise me you'll stay."

"I can't promise that," she argues, and I want to kiss her but she pushes me down on the bed and I'm too unsteady to not fall backward, plopping down on the bed.

She leaves the room and that's the last thing that I remember from that night.

34

KENNA

I don't know what the hell is going on with Derek and I tell myself I can't really worry about that now. I can't care. It'd only hurt me more later. I leave him half-coherent in his bedroom and go to start Maggie's shower and run Eli a bath in his room while I walk back and forth in the hallway to check on each of them. Maggie likes her privacy but Eli's still young enough he gets afraid in the tub by himself, so it's a little work.

I'm used to it, though, because I usually bathe them before Derek gets home from work. My heart aches when Eli says "Mama, out," and holds up his wet arms to me as I hold the towel.

I smile at him, and when I deposit him in his bed, he's sucking his thumb, which Derek and I have almost broken him of. He's regressed a bit since he's been sick, though, and I don't want to scold him.

"Eli, why do you call me Mama?" I ask him softly, and Eli tilts his head, looking confused.

"Because you are my Mama," he says simply. "You do all the things mamas are supposed to do."

"Like what?" I ask, my heart aching.

"You take care of me," he says. "You play with me and tell me you love me and that I'm doing a good job. My friend at pre-school says that's what good mamas do. You're a good mama, Kenna."

I stare at him for a moment, my eyes watering, before I sniffle.

"Thank you, Eli. You're a good kid."

He grins at me. "I know. Will you tell me a story?"

I tell him a thrilling tale about robot train conductors and he falls asleep in the middle of it. Maggie takes longer to go to sleep, asking me to lie down with her, and I do, having missed her. She puts her head on my shoulder and we both drift off. I finally wake up and disentangle myself, thinking I should go check on Derek.

With the amount of beer he put back before and during dinner, plus the three hamburgers he ate, he's likely to throw up all over himself.

I peek in the door and I think he's sleeping until he calls to me.

"Sweetheart?"

My heart sinks. *Sweetheart.* Not Kenna.

My heartrate speeds up as I walk into the room.

"Close the door," he orders, and he sounds a bit more sober, so I do, walking toward the bed. Derek turns on the lamp, squinting at me.

"The kids asleep?" he asks, his voice hoarse from sleep and alcohol.

I nod slowly. "They went down okay. Maggie had trouble sleeping, so I laid down with her a bit."

Derek looks up at me. "I meant what I said, you know?"

"What do you mean?" I ask, biting my lip.

He leans up and reaches out to me, tugging me into bed

and subsequently, into his lap, nuzzling against my neck from behind.

"I don't want you to go."

"What does that *mean,* Derek?" I ask, sighing but leaning against him. I can't ever seem to tell him no, no matter what happens.

"You know what it means," he says simply, pushing my hair back from my throat and kissing me there, making me moan in the back of my throat.

It's been a while since he's touched me like this, and I can't deny that I like it, that I crave it.

"I want to be the only man who ever touches you," he says, reaching around to shove his hand down my shorts, pressing his fingers against my clit.

I gasp and rock back against him, feeling him hard against my ass.

"You are," I say.

"Not for long," he mutters miserably, and kisses my throat again, sucking there to make a mark.

"Derek," I whimper, not sure what I'm asking for, but he pushes his fingers deeper, hooking two inside me so that I breathe out his name again.

"Don't go," he says again, a whisper against my throat, and I don't know how to answer him. I don't know how to tell him I have to go, because he doesn't want me and I'm growing his baby in my stomach as we speak and I don't want that to be the reason that makes him ask me to be with him or the reason that finally pulls him away for good.

I don't know how to tell him that I've been in love with him for months and I want to be part of his family. I'm terrified that he'll reject me again, so I don't say anything, just let him touch me, one hand kneading my breasts, the other cupped against my sex.

He rocks his hips against me in a low groan and then removes his fingers, flipping me over onto the bed. He tugs down my shorts impatiently and he's removed his shirt at some point in the night so I spread my hands across his broad chest.

Derek growls in the back of his throat, shoving down his sweats to press into me, slowly at first and then rolling his hips in a steady pace that makes my breath hitch in my chest.

With each thrust, his pelvic bone hits my clitoris, and I'm arching my back and crying out when he starts to move faster.

"All mine," he murmurs, and my eyes snap open, looking into his lust-filled green ones. "You're all mine, sweetheart."

"Am I?" I ask, and he nods, biting his lip and focusing at where he's pumping in and out of me. I tremble all over when I come, digging my nails into his shoulders and he groans as I clench around him, his thrusts getting sloppy.

"Fuck, wanted this to last longer," he mourns, but it's only a few more strokes before he's spilling inside me, his seed dripping down my thighs. I expect him to go cold now, shut down like he's done so many times before, but after he pulls out, when I try to get out of bed, he grabs my hip bone tight in one hand. "Stay," he commands, and I don't know if he means just for now or if he means forever, but I can't say no.

I've never been able to say no to Derek Ledderman. I wiggle back against him and he puts both arms around me, pulling me close and pressing his face against the back of my neck.

"It makes me crazy to think of you with someone else," he admits.

"You're territorial," I accuse.

He's quiet for a moment. "It's normal to be territorial over something you might lose," he argues.

I hitch in a breath. "You're not losing me. You don't want me," I say, and he's so quiet that I think he's dropped off to sleep.

"I've never said I didn't want you," he murmurs against my skin. "That's not the problem."

"Then what is?" I ask, desperate. I want him to tell me *why* we can't be together, why I can't be part of this family.

"You'll leave me," he insists. "You'll meet someone else and you'll go and I won't be able to handle it."

"You don't trust me," I say flatly, turning to face him, and he bites his lip, his green eyes dark with some emotion I can't name.

"I don't trust anybody. I can't afford to," he says softly, and I want to kiss him, want to tell him that he can trust *me*, that it'll all be okay, that I'll never leave him, but I can see he's made his decision.

"Then I have to go," I say shakily. Derek slumps, his face falling.

"When?"

"Two weeks," I say. The semester will be starting in three weeks and I'll take a week to get settled back in on campus.

"Two weeks," he parrots back in a hollow voice. "When will you tell the kids?"

"End of the week," I say softly. "I'll talk to them myself."

Derek's arms loosen around me and I wiggle out of them, standing up and finding my shorts, tugging them back on over my bikini bottoms.

"I'm going to take a shower and go to bed," I say, and Derek doesn't answer. When I turn back he has his forearm thrown over his eyes, breathing hard.

I swallow hard and head back to my room, undressing and getting into the shower before I burst into tears.

When I finish crying and washing myself, I call my best friend, Cherie. She's the only one who knows the truth about my pregnancy, and I need someone to talk to.

"What's wrong?" she answers, and I realize it's almost midnight.

"Sorry to call so late," I say in a husky voice.

"You've been crying. Kenna, what is it?" she asks with concern in her voice. "Do you need me to come get you?"

"No," I assure her. "I'm watching the kids. Derek got drunk tonight and I had to put him to bed."

Cherie scoffs. "I guess he's not taking you going back to college very well."

"Hardly," I admit. "I didn't think that he was going to take it this hard. I think he just doesn't want to be alone again with the kids."

Cherie pauses. "Do you really think that's it, Kenna?"

I sigh. "I don't know. What am I supposed to think?"

"That he's in love with you. That he's just got too much damage to admit it."

"Do you think so?" I ask hesitantly, and Cherie scoffs.

"Yeah, I think so. You've always wanted a family, right? Now you're part of one, and you're even having his baby. Don't you think that would change things?"

"I don't want it to change things," I say stubbornly. "I want him to want me because he loves me, not because I'm pregnant."

"You don't think he loves you? After all this time?"

"I don't know," I say hoarsely. "I wish I did."

"You have to tell him about the baby, Kenna," she says in a low voice. "Sooner rather than later."

"I know."

"It's going to be okay," she says firmly. "Either way."

I sniffle. "Thanks, Cher."

"Anytime."

We hang up after another few moments and I lie face down on the bed in my robe, sighing up at the ceiling. My skin feels all pruny since I'd cried for so long in the shower. Maybe I should tell Derek about the baby before I leave after all.

35

DEREK

I don't feel hungover when I wake up, so I suspect that I'm still a little drunk and take an Uber to work instead of my car. I'm sure I look like shit despite my shower and new suit, and I'm half asleep during the first sales meeting of the day.

Grayson's there just to observe, and afterwards, he asks me into his office.

I roll my eyes. "Am in in trouble or something?"

Grayson stares at me and then just goes into his office. I follow with a sigh.

"What the hell is going on with you, Derek?" he asks after I close the door.

I run my hand through my hair. "Nothing," I mutter.

"You look hungover. You don't drink like that," Grayson argues back. "Is it the nanny?"

"Of course it's the nanny," I mutter, sitting down across from him. "She's leaving."

"And you don't want her to go?"

"God, no," I say. "And not just because of the kids."

Grayson nods. "You're in love with her."

I freeze and my throat feels tight, but I know that he's right. "Fuck. Yeah, I am," I admit.

"So tell her," he says.

I groan. "How do I do that? I've rejected her over and over, and I still don't know if I can be the man she deserves."

"You think I'm the man that Lilian deserves?" Grayson asks dryly. "You think I've got it all together, that I don't even think about when she left? I'm afraid all the time that it'll happen again."

I look at him. "Really?"

"Of course. Love is hard, Derek. It's scary. There's so many ways it can go wrong. But if you really feel that way toward Kenna, you've got to tell her. You'll regret it the rest of your life if you don't."

"I'm sorry about the meeting," I mumble.

Grayson waves his hand. "It's not like I'm going to fire you. Not only are you my close friend but you're the best damn salesperson in the tri-county area. Oh, yeah, and you own some shares in the company," he mocks me

"Still. I shouldn't be coming to work when I'm fucked up like this. My mind is all over the place," I admit.

"Well, we've all done it," Grayson jokes, referring to after Lilian left when he was a mess for months.

We hadn't been talking at that time, but I'd heard stories of Grayson coming in shit-faced. He was lucky that his father owned the company.

"How do I tell her?" I ask, feeling lost, and Grayson raises an eyebrow.

"You sit her down and tell her. It's simple."

"It doesn't feel very simple," I mutter.

Grayson laughs. "Well, whatever you do, don't drink the night you tell her. She'll think it's just the booze."

I nod slowly. "You're right." A headache is forming at my

temples. "I don't want to drink anymore anyway. Too old to be shit-faced," I groan, and Grayson laughs.

"That's right, old man," he teases, and I reach over to punch him in the arm lightly.

By the time I get back to my office, there's not much work to do. I'm taking out some clients later in the week, but for now there's just commission paperwork for myself and my team, and I fill it out quickly.

It's only about four in the afternoon, but I figure I only get so much time with Kenna, so I go home and she's standing outside by the pool, watching the kids paddle around.

I'm determined to tell her after the kids go to bed, and she stays outside for a while before taking Eli to bathe him. I stop her, taking him from her.

"I got it," I say. "You relax. You just got out of the hospital."

She stares at me for a moment but then nods and hands Eli over, who only whines a little.

Maggie takes her shower with the door open while Eli splashes around in his bathroom, and Maggie goes down easy. Eli, however, wants a story from Kenna.

"It's just me tonight, honey. Kenna's resting."

Eli's green eyes widen. "Is she sick again?"

"No," I say easily. "She just needs to rest because she was sick before. Just like you."

"She could rest in my room," he says slyly, and I laugh.

"I think she'd prefer her own bed, bud."

"But I miss Mama," he whines, lying down and pulling the covers up, and my heart aches.

"You know Kenna isn't really your mama, right, Eli?" I ask gently.

Eli peeks out from under the covers. "Why not? Can't she be? You could marry her."

I froze. "You want me to marry Kenna?"

Maggie had brought it up before, but never Eli.

Eli nods eagerly. "Yeah. Then she could be here all the time and take care of us!"

"I don't know if she wants to marry me," I mumble.

"Did you ask her?" he asks, as if in a scolding tone, and I chuckle.

"No. No, I haven't asked her."

"Well, then *ask* her, Daddy," he says as if I'm stupid, and I smile and kiss his forehead.

"I'll think about it," I say. "You get some rest, little man."

Eli nods and closes his eyes and I sigh, walking out of his room and half-shutting the door.

Kenna's standing in the hallway, looking at me wide-eyed.

"Derek, I need to talk to you," she says.

"I need to talk to you, too," I say back, feeling nervous. A flush heats my cheeks.

"Let's go out by the pool," she suggests, and I follow her downstairs and out onto the deck.

She sits down on one of the lawn chairs and doesn't face me, staring straight ahead.

"Is this about you leaving?" I ask softly.

"Kind of," she admits, glancing at me out of the corner of her eye.

She steadies herself by bracing herself on the chair and I frown.

"Are you feeling okay?"

She shakes her head. "Not really."

"Then we don't have to talk about this right now," I say

firmly, not sure if I'm glad to get out of it but not wanting to upset her by confessing while she's ill.

"We have to," she whispers, but she's gone so pale that I stand up and scoop her into my arms. She squeaks but holds on, her arms around my neck as I carry her back into the house.

I take her upstairs into her room and she leans her head against my chest as if she's exhausted.

"Maybe I swam too much with the kids," she murmurs, and I hum in the back of my throat and deposit her down on the bed, kissing her temple.

"Get some rest," I say, even though it's only eight. "You need to heal and get better."

Kenna nods slightly and closes her eyes, and I hate that I haven't told her, but she needs to get better. She doesn't need extra stress.

What if she's angry with me? What if she hates me now? There are so many possibilities, and only a few of them good.

What do I think is going to happen? That she's just going to agree to be with me even though I've rejected her, even though I made love to her just last night and then told her I don't trust her? I hate myself.

I've been sending her mixed signals for weeks, and I can see that now. I didn't mean to, but I had, and no wonder she wants to leave.

How would it feel if she'd done that to me? Kenna has always been clear about what she wants, and she wants me. She wants this family.

And now, I don't know if I can convince her to be a part of it.

36

KENNA

I don't know why I began to feel so ill out at the pool, but I guess it probably had something to do with what I had to tell Derek. I'm nervous as all hell, and I don't know how to say it.

I'm pregnant and I know you don't want me or trust me, but can we be a family?

I scoff at the thought, rolling over in bed. As I lie there, I start to feel worse and worse and finally have to run to the bathroom, throwing up.

After I vomit, I sit down on the toilet to pee, and when I wipe, I look at the tissue, shocked. *Blood.*

It's dark red, and my heart jumps into my throat. I'm terrified. The *baby.*

I think that I shouldn't drive myself but I've been lying in bed, not sleeping, for hours, and it's after midnight.

I swallow hard and walk to Derek's bedroom, opening the door and knocking on the doorjamb.

Derek sits up quickly, rubbing at his eyes. "Kenna? Is it one of the kids?"

Yes, technically, I think, but I don't say it.

"I need you to drive me to the hospital," I say firmly, and Derek stands up, pulling on a shirt and a pair of sweats quickly.

"What's going on?" he asks, and I shake my head.

"I don't know, but I'm bleeding."

Derek looks at me like I'm *very* naïve, and part of me wants to hit him. "Like...your period?"

His face is flushed.

"Worse," I say. "Listen, I just need you to take me. I'm sorry but I shouldn't be driving like this—"

"What's going on, Kenna? Are you feeling a neckache again?" he asks, sliding on his flipflops.

Derek grabs Maggie in one arm and Eli in the other and rushes with them to the car. They're both still sleeping when he straps them in.

"I'll call my Mom to come get them," he mutters as he slides into the driver's side, glancing at me now and again on the ride to the hospital. He calls his mother on the way and she agrees to come and pick them up.

She makes it there before we do, since she lives closer to the hospital, and takes the sleepy kids to put into her car.

Derek follows me into the hospital and stands up when they call me back.

"Not yet," I tell him. "I'll call if I need you." I don't want him to know about the baby if this pregnancy falls through. It would only hurt him, and I'm already hurting for the both of us, no need for him to be upset for something that almost happened.

Derek frowns, but sits back down.

As soon as I'm in the back and the physician's assistant comes in, I blurt out, "I'm eleven weeks pregnant, I just got released two days ago due to meningitis, and now I'm bleeding."

The young woman leaves the room and brings back in an ultrasound machine and a fetal heartbeat monitor, and my heart is in my throat while she searches for the heartbeat with the wand. It seems to take her forever to find it and I just know I'm going to scream, but finally the whooshing sound of the baby's heartbeat sounds in my ears.

I sigh in relief.

"Baby seems okay," she says gently. "Sometimes there's a bit of spotting, especially after some more extenuating activity or sexual intercourse."

I groan inwardly. I should have known. I feel stupid and at the verge of tears.

"Your husband is asking about you. Should I bring him back?" she asks, and I nod tiredly, not explaining that he's technically just my boss and also, the baby's father.

I don't want to get into that with a stranger when I haven't even told him.

Derek hurries into the room after the doctor leaves, and I don't even bother hiding the fetal monitor. At this point, I have to tell him.

He doesn't seem to notice, sitting next to me immediately and taking my hand.

"Is it the meningitis?" he asks worriedly.

I shake my head. "No, just...stress," I say vaguely, and Derek's green eyes look so concerned that I can't stop myself from crying.

"Kenna, what's wrong?" he asks softly. "Are you in pain?"

"No," I sniffle. "I just...I need to tell you something, Derek."

"Anything," he says, leaning down to kiss my knuckles, and that just makes me cry harder.

I gesture over to the fetal monitor, showing him the heartbeat.

"What...what's that?" he asks hesitantly.

"It's your baby's heartbeat," I say hoarsely, and Derek freezes, staring at the monitor.

"My..." he trails off. "Our baby?"

I nod, struggling not to start sobbing. I wipe the tears that have started streaming down my face. "This is why I have to leave," I manage. "This is why I have to go so soon."

Derek doesn't speak, of course he doesn't.

I'm sure he's shocked but he knows that the best thing is for me to go. He knows that I can't be part of this family.

He stands awkwardly, just staring for a moment.

"The baby, it's...it's healthy?" he asks, his voice shaking.

I nod. "Yeah, the baby's okay," I assure him softly, and I expect him to say something else but he doesn't. He just nods and walks out of the room.

I start crying in earnest then, holding the covers up to cover my face, and the nurse comes in to give me some nausea medication. She asks me if I'm in pain and I shake my head.

I am, but it's nothing that can be helped with medication.

I think about calling my mother to come and see me but I don't want her finding out that Derek's the father. He left when he found out, so that probably means I'm on my own, right? Instead, I call the only person that will help me. The one that know everything. Cherie.

She's asleep when I call but she gets there within fifteen minutes, sitting by my bedside as I cry. She holds my hand, looking at me sympathetically.

"He just left," I sob, and Cherie's hand tightens on mine.

"Maybe he just needs some time," she says softly.

"Or he doesn't want me and he's ready for me to go," I wail, and Cherie leans over to hug me.

"Even if he does, you've got your parents and you've got me," she says. "I promise that we'll be here for you."

"I know," I say gratefully, hugging her back, and finally, she pulls away, looking at me.

"Do you want me to try and find him?"

"No, that looks desperate," I mutter, and Cherie laughs.

"You're pregnant, Ken. I think that's past being desperate."

"Well, I don't want him to come back unless he wants to," I argue, and Cherie rolls her eyes.

"Stubborn."

"Very," I agree, smiling a little and wiping at my eyes again. "Ugh, I'm so tired of crying. Never get pregnant, Cherie."

She chuckles. "I don't plan on it. That's why I have like thirty tests in my bathroom," she jokes, and I laugh shakily.

"Thank you for coming," I say, truly grateful, and Cherie smiles.

"I'll stay as long as you like, but you're going to have to let me go get some coffee."

"Of course, go," I say, waving my hand. "Just come back."

Cherie laughs. "I will."

She leaves the room and I put the pillow over my face, breathing into it and wanting to scream. Derek leaving shows he doesn't want me. He doesn't want this baby. Right?

I mean, he made that clear a long time ago, and it's even clearer now.

So, what am I going to do?

Cherie returns with coffee for herself and decaf for me.

I make a face.

"They say caffeine is bad for babies," she says, and I look down at my stomach, rubbing over the slight swell. I'm starting to get a little pouch, and I guess Derek would have found out sooner rather than later.

"I've always wanted a baby," I mumble. "But I never thought it would be like this."

"It doesn't matter how you got the baby," Cherie assures me. "It's yours now, and we'll help you take care of it."

I smile softly. "I know. I'm not alone." I sigh. "I guess I'll go back to school next week and go from there."

Cherie cracks a smile. "I think Derek will stop you, but that's just my prediction."

"Don't give me hope, Cherie," I warn, but she just shrugs.

"I saw him downstairs pacing around the cafeteria," she says. "At least I think it's him. Tall, green eyes, graying blond hair?"

"That's him," I say, my eyes wide. "He's still at the hospital?"

Cherie nods. "I bet he'll be back any minute."

"What am I going to say to him?" I groan, and Cherie laughs. "You've already told him everything, right?"

"Everything but that I love him," I say, and Cherie snorts.

"He already knows that."

I hit her weakly with the heel of my hand.

Then there's a knock on the doorjamb, and I freeze.

Cherie stands up as Derek walks in with a bouquet of flowers he's obviously gotten from the gift shop, and a onesie that says I Love L.A. with a heart in the middle.

I can't help but laugh through my tears when he hands it to me.

My heart is in my throat as Cherie leaves, and I look up at Derek with wide eyes.

37

DEREK

I pace around downstairs for about an hour, freaking out. Kenna's pregnant. It's mine. I'm the only one that's ever touched her and now she's carrying my child. My *third* child. *Our* child.

She's been carrying this secret for god knows how long, and I've just been playing with her feelings. I feel like the world's biggest asshole. No wonder she didn't tell me. *I* wouldn't tell me.

It's complicated, how I feel about Kenna. I love her; I know that now, but I also know that she deserves better. I know that she's young and free and she doesn't deserve to be tied down to an old man with two kids and a bunch of baggage.

But now that she's pregnant...

I really have to tell her. I have to tell her how I feel and I have to tell her now, before she disappears to Washington and I lose out on my chance to make her happy and also to be a good father.

I think I know that she has feelings for me, but there's

always the possibility that she won't forgive me. Hell, if I was in her shoes, I don't know if I would forgive myself.

I go down to the giftshop and pace around there for a while, looking at the flowers and the baby clothes. I pick out a green unisex onesie, the only one they have, and there's a cheesy saying on it but I don't even notice.

There's only one thing left to do, and I'm dreading it.

I walk into her hospital room and her friend gives me a smile and leaves, and when I hand Kenna the gifts, she laughs even though there are tears streaming down her cheeks.

"Kenna," I breathe, sitting next to her. "I'm so sorry."

She tilts her head. "What are you sorry for?"

"So many things," I mutter, not knowing how to elaborate.

"What does that mean, Derek? You don't....you don't want this baby?"

I blink at her. "Of course I want this baby."

"But you don't want me," she says flatly.

I run a hand through my hair. "Marry me," I say suddenly, having no idea what I'm saying, just speaking off the top of my head.

Kenna snorts. "I'm not marrying you just because I'm pregnant."

I frown. "Why not?"

"Because I don't want to get married because I'm *pregnant*, Derek," she says, sounding exasperated. "I'm only going to get married once, and I'm marrying for love."

Wouldn't you be marrying for love? I thought. *Don't you feel the same way I do?*

But the words won't come out. I don't know how to say it. I'm afraid to say it. I don't want her to tell me that she's fallen out of love with me because of everything I've done.

"I want to be this baby's father," I say finally, and Kenna's face falls. She looks away and fingers the bottom of the onesie.

"You will be," she says softly. "You can come with me to the ultrasounds and I'll give you updates while I'm in college."

"You're still going to college? In Washington?" I say incredulously, and Kenna frowns.

"It's for my career," she says.

"You can have a career *here*. You can go to Berkeley," I say stubbornly.

"I don't *want* to go to Berkeley," she says stubbornly. "I want to go back to college with my friends."

I freeze. "What friends? Are you seeing someone there?"

Kenna rolls her eyes. "Of course that's what you'd think," she mutters.

"Well, are you?"

There are too many emotions whirling around in me and I know I'm being irrational but I can't believe she's still leaving. I can't let her leave with my baby in her belly, but how am I going to stop her?

"Is it any of your business?" she snaps.

"You said I was the first one to touch you," I grumble, jealousy raging through me.

"You *were*. You *are*." She sounds exasperated. "But that doesn't mean you'll be the only one to touch me."

"What if I want to be the only one?" I demand. "What if I want *you*?"

"You want me? You want all of me? Want to let me be part of this family?" Kenna asks, looking up at me defiantly.

Yes. I think. *Yes, that's exactly what I want*.

But the words stick in my throat because I can't stop thinking about what it was like when I walked in my home and I just *knew* Suzanna was gone. I could feel the lack of her presence in the air, somehow, and sure enough, when I walked upstairs to our bedroom, all her things were gone. And what if it happened with Kenna? It would kill me. I already feel so much more for her than I ever did for Suzanna. I wouldn't be able to handle it if she left me.

"You can't even answer me," Kenna says brokenly, and I hate myself. I hate myself for being afraid, for not knowing my own feelings until it's too late.

"I'm sorry," I choke out, and leave the room.

I'm an idiot. I came here to tell her that I love her. I came here to tell her that I want her, and I ended up doing the exact opposite.

She's never going to forgive me. I'm going to be alone forever, and have a child that I barely see because she'll meet some guy in Washington, have love and light in her life, and I'll be alone.

I'm fucking up my one chance at happiness, and for what? Because I can't get over what Suzanna did? Because I can't bring myself to be happy again?

And god, the kids. They love her so much. How am I supposed to tell them that I messed this up? That Kenna is leaving because of me?

I stalk to the car and slam my hands down on the steering wheel over and over, yelling out my anger and hurt and frustration.

Kenna's not the one who broke my heart. I did it to myself.

I just keep pacing around the hospital, not sure what to do. I know that I won't be given any information about her condition, just like before. Dawn is breaking by the time I can make myself leave the hospital.

Mom is at home watching the kids so I go to the office, trying my best not to slam the door behind me.

Grayson's on vacation with Lilian and the kids, starting today, so I don't even have anyone to talk to. I try to throw myself into work, but Kenna is all I think about all day.

When I return home, my mother leaves almost immediately, complaining about her arthritis, and I feel guilty for leaving her with the kids for so long.

Eli walks up to me, looking up at me with big green eyes.

"When is Mama getting better?" he asks immediately, and I sigh and pick him up.

"She's doing okay. Just has to spend a day or so in the hospital."

"Can we go see her?"

"Maybe later," I say vaguely.

Maggie's coloring on a pad on the floor. "I'm making Kenna another card," she says matter-of-factly, and it sends a pang through my heart.

I guess I'll have to sit down with them and explain they're having a brother or sister that they'll barely see. I don't know how to tell them now, though, so I just go through the motions of bathing them and putting them to bed.

I get them off to sleep and go into my room, sitting down hard on the edge of the bed and covering my face with my hands. I feel so much that it's hard to even process things.

What the hell am I doing?

38

KENNA

I want to scream when Derek leaves the hospital room, but instead, I just cry, rolling up in a fetal position. By the time I get myself together, it's nearing daylight.

I feel so alone that I don't know what to do with myself.

Derek hasn't told me that he wants me. He's only told me that he wants this baby, which is fine, since the baby is as much his as it is mine. But while it is inside me, it gets to go with me everywhere. I don't want to deprive him of anything, but I won't force him either, so if he chose to leave me here, I can only assume he is done with me for now. Or at least until the baby is born.

So, I can just go back to Washington like I planned. Not because I'm seeing anybody, like Derek accused, but because I want to be around friends and I don't want to be around Derek Ledderman and his beautiful family that I can never be a true part of.

When I saw Derek with that onesie, my heart just about melted. I hoped he would give it to me and tell me that he loved me, tell me that he wanted me and the baby both, but instead I got a half-assed forced proposal and no real emotions. Derek can't open up to me, and I don't know if that's because of his past or because he simply doesn't feel the same way that I do. Though he didn't quite contradict me when I mentioned it would be a loveless marriage, so that should be my answer right there.

I spend another two days in the hospital for observation, but everything turns out fine and I'm discharged after crying alone in my hospital room for the better part of that time. My parents visit, and even my brother and sister, but I still feel alone.

I guess it's because I know this is almost a glimpse at my future. Me, alone with my baby, occasionally my family around to say hi and visit for a minute or two, and then back to just being me and the bean, even if Derek is a part of its life.

I'm trembling when my mother drops me off at Derek's.

"Ken, are you okay?" she asks as she pulls into the gate.

"Fine," I tell her with a plastered-on smile. "Just still a little weak and shaky."

"You get in there and get some rest," she orders me. "I know the kids will be happy to see you but you make sure to take care of yourself and my grandbaby."

I chuckle, patting her hand before opening the car door. "I will, Mom."

Maggie meets me at the door with her drawings and cards that she's made me, three of them in different colors and with different pictures.

I ooh and ahh over them and Eli abruptly tries to show her up by bringing his own drawing, a scribbled mess that I pretend is the prettiest picture in the universe.

The way they beam at me makes my heart shatter all over again.

Derek must have taken the day off work, because he's in the kitchen, making lunch for the kids.

"Do you want something to eat?" he asks in a flat tone.

"Sure," I answer, and in a few moments, he brings lunch into the living room, which he never does. The kids sit next to me, me in the middle between them, and Derek sits in the recliner across from us.

He won't even look at me.

After lunch, I go up to take a nap and sleep a few thin hours. When I wake up, it's time for the kids to go to bed and I tuck them both in, kissing Eli's cheek and wrapping Maggie tightly the way she likes.

"Snug as a bug in a rug," I tell her, and she gives me a smile. She's lost a tooth since the last time I'd seen her. "Did the tooth fairy come to see you?" I ask, and she nods happily.

"Gave me five bucks," she says proudly.

"Geez," I marvel. "I only ever got a dollar."

"Maybe my teeth are special."

I laugh. "Probably. You are a very special little girl."

I stand up, but Maggie grabs my hand, tugging me back. "Kenna?"

"What is it, sweetie?"

"You know how Eli calls you Mama?"

I nod, swallowing hard.

"Would you be mad if I called you Mama too?"

My heart aches so much I feel like I'm dying, and I lean down and kiss her forehead.

"You can call me whatever you want," I assure her, and she closes her eyes, smiling.

I'm fighting tears when I go downstairs for a glass of water and Derek is in the kitchen, eating peanut butter on graham crackers with milk, just in a pair of sweats, his chest bare.

I try not to look at him.

I don't know what to say. I want to put off leaving as long as possible. I don't want to tell those kids that I'm leaving them. I don't want them to feel abandoned like their mother, my aunt, abandoned them. But deep down, the real reason is that I don't want to leave at all.

I expect Derek to leave. I figure he'll pad back upstairs and leave me down there alone. I go into the fridge for a bottle of water and suddenly his arms wrap around my waist from behind, his face pressing into the side of my neck.

"Do you have to go?" he asks softly, and I can't help leaning back against him. Derek Ledderman is my weakness, and I can't deny that, not even to myself.

"I do," I say, just as softly.

"Can I kiss you goodbye?"

I take in a hitched breath as he places a kiss on my shoulder, moving aside my T-shirt.

I turn toward him, looking up into his sea-green eyes and there's an expression on his face I don't recognize, something like hurt.

Why would he be hurt? He's the one that doesn't want me.

Derek doesn't say anything, always being a man of few words, just leans down and kisses me, soft and sweet.

I'm the one who deepens the kiss, makes it more searching.

The way he's clutching at me making my body heat up.

Derek groans into my mouth, picking me up on the counter and suddenly I'm glad that I'm wearing a sundress.

Derek puts his hands on my breasts, kneading them

through the fabric, palming along my peaked nipples and my back arches, my thighs parting so that he stands between them. He grabs me under my ass and thighs and pulls me closer to the edge, rolling his hips up against my core and I gasp, wrapping my arms around his neck.

"I want to be the only man to touch you, at least one more time," he murmurs, and his eyes are hot and searching my face as if I might say no.

As if I could ever say no to him.

"Derek," I breathe, and he grunts, moving the crotch of my panties to one side so that he can slide his fingers along my lower lips, dipping two of them inside of me until I'm panting and trying not to moan too loudly.

It's a big house, and it's unlikely the kids will hear me, but still, I don't want any surprises. We already have to explain that I'm leaving. I don't want to have another conversation with them about what we're doing in the kitchen.

I reach between us to grope him through his sweats and Derek groans softly, thrusting into my hand.

"You see what you do to me? How hard you make me?" he says under his breath, and it makes heat pool in my lower abdomen, makes me feel hot all over.

Derek pulls down his sweats and shifts to slide into me, grunting impatiently as he moves my panties aside again, and it takes a moment to get the right angle but when he does, I want to cry out.

He clamps his hand over my mouth, and I breathe through my nose, the action somehow making me hotter.

He thrusts up into me in long, slow strokes, as if he could do this all night and my thighs are already trembling.

I dig my nails into his shoulders, and he groans, dropping his hand and kissing me again and making the sound into my mouth. I don't want this to end but I'm approaching my orgasm quickly and I let out a low whine, muffled by Derek's mouth.

"Quiet, sweetheart," he says in a low tone. "Don't want the kids to wake up."

I nod eagerly and rock my hips forward as he continues to fuck me, harder now, less rhythm, and when I cum, I just dig my nails deeper into his shoulders, clawing down his back and Derek moans louder than I have been.

I smirk, unable to help myself. "Who can't be quiet now?"

"You drive me crazy," Derek mutters, his eyes hot as he looks into mine and keeps fucking me, watching my face instead of where we're joined together, and I'm at the verge of another orgasm again when he spills inside me.

I tremble, thinking it's over, that he's going to go back upstairs and leave me panting on the counter, but instead, he pulls out and presses his fingers back into me, as if keeping his seed inside.

I lick my lips, feeling hot all over again, and coming a second time as he pumps his fingers into me, pressing his thumb against my clit.

It's probably the best orgasm I've ever had, and I have to stop myself from screaming by biting into my lip so hard it bleeds.

Derek looks at me and my bloody lip and thumbs the blood off it, popping it into his mouth after and keeping eye contact with me.

"Derek," I gasp, tears suddenly threatening at the backs of my eyes. "Do you want me to go?"

"No," he says hoarsely. "I don't *ever* want you to go."

"What does that mean?" I ask as he pulls his fingers out of me, looking at me intently.

"What do you think it means, Kenna? It means I want you. It means...I love you."

"Wh-what?" I stare at him, shell-shocked. "Really?"

He chuckles, rubbing his hand across his face. "Of course, really. I've been going crazy thinking about you leaving. I can't even imagine it."

"Because I might meet other guys?"

"Because I can't live without you," he says, searching my face. "Because I don't know how to do this without you, sweetheart."

"I-I don't understand," I stutter.

"Marry me, Kenna Lodge," he says, still pinning me up against the counter, his arms loosely around my waist. "Marry me, not because you are pregnant, not because of anything other than the fact that we love each other, and let's raise this family together."

I don't answer, completely flabbergasted. I never expected him to open up this much to me. I never expected him to say these things.

"I know that I have a lot to work on," Derek says. "I know that I've been afraid, a coward, and that I've not trusted you, but I'll change, Kenna. I promise. I want to make you happy."

"You do make me happy," I say shakily.

"Then will you do it? Will you marry me?"

I tilt my chin up. "I'm still going back to college."

"Berkeley?" he asks hopefully, and I crack a smile and nod.

Derek picks me up off the counter, squeezing me in a bear hug. "So, you'll marry me?"

"I guess I'll marry a rich old man," I tease, giggling, my heart feeling fuller than ever before.

Then he kisses me, thoroughly, and we stay downstairs

in the kitchen and talk all night, until the kids get up the next morning.

"Mama?" Eli says, rubbing his eyes as he pads into the kitchen.

I turn toward him with a big smile. "Go get your sister," I say excitedly. "Your dad and I have news."

I turn to Derek, thinking maybe I'm being too exuberant, but he's grinning from ear to ear.

"Is it Christmas?" Eli asks when he walks into the kitchen and Maggie scoffs.

"Christmas is *months* away," she says. Then looks at the both of us and asks, "Right?"

Derek laughs.

"It feels like Christmas to me," he says, taking my hand.

Maggie's eyes widen. "Are you finally marrying Kenna?"

"I am," Derek says, kissing my knuckles, and both the kids jump around and cheer.

"One more thing," I say, holding Eli in my lap.

He looks up at me with wide eyes.

"You're going to have a baby brother or sister."

Maggie groans. "Oh, *no*, not another brother," she whines, and we all break into a laugh together.

I've never been happier in my life.

39

DEREK

Kenna's parents take the news better than I expected, although they're confused at first. My mother tells me she always knew something was going on with that nanny of mine, and I can't help but laugh.

Everyone's at the wedding, even Logan, although he's circling around Meredith like a shark, and I'm not sure what's going on with the two of them.

Grayson is my best man and Logan and Loxton are groomsmen, and Kenna makes Maggie a flower girl while Eli is the ring-bearer.

Cherie, her maid of honor, has a twinkle in her eyes when she tells me that she knew I'd come around.

When Kenna comes down the aisle, glowing with her belly swollen with my baby, I almost lose it, wiping tears from my eyes. This is the second time I've been married but this is different. This is *wonderful,* and it feels like I'm doing it for the first time.

Kenna pouts at the reception.

"I can't believe I'm getting married without champagne," she whines.

I laugh. "I got some bubbly apple cider for you."

Her blue eyes light up. "Really?"

I pour her a glass, clinking it with my own. "I'm not drinking, either."

I want to be clear. I want to remember this day for the rest of my life.

Frank, Kenna's father, was a bit skeptical at first, because of the age difference and all my baggage, but he knows I'm a good husband and a good father, since, of course, I was married to his sister.

"You take care of her and my grandchild," he says firmly after the daddy and daughter dance, and there are still tears streaking down his face.

"I will," I promise.

The wedding was beautiful, the reception was a hit and I spared no expense on the honeymoon either.

It's not quite a traditional honeymoon.

We take the kids to Disneyland, and Maggie and Eli fight the whole way there.

"Remind me why we did this again?" I say, frustrated, and Kenna just giggles.

"Because we love our kids and we want to be with them all the time," she says.

"Promise me we get a wedding night just to ourselves when we get home," I growl, and Kenna smiles and puts her hand on my knee.

"I've already talked to my parents about it," she says under her breath as Eli screams that Maggie stole his dinosaur.

"You don't even *like* dinosaurs, Maggie, please," I groan, and Kenna pats my knee.

"Let's sing a song, kids," she suggests, and then the sounds of 'Wheels on the Bus' ring in my ears as we make the rest of the drive.

It's a lot better than their screaming. Kenna is still amazing with the kids.

Maggie started calling her Mama, like Eli, the day we told them we were getting married.

We haven't found out the sex of the baby yet because Kenna wants it to be a surprise, but Maggie is praying that it's a girl instead of a boy. Kenna and I don't care either way, as long as they're healthy, of course.

Secretly, I hope it's a little girl that looks just like my beautiful wife.

Eli and Maggie run around the resort for a few hours while Kenna and I get settled, unpacking everything.

She winces a bit when she picks up the luggage and I take it from her immediately.

"You aren't supposed to be picking anything up," I scold, and Kenna scoffs.

"It's just a bag," she mutters, but I don't let her do any of the other unpacking.

When we're all settled, the kids are chomping at the bit to go to Disneyland and Kenna's a little grumpy because she's hungry.

We eat at a Disney themed pizza restaurant and take lots of pictures. Eli has his tongue out in nearly all of them.

By the time we get to the rides, Kenna's less grumpy but still pouty because she can't ride any of the rides.

Eli and Maggie run off to the teacups and I wait with Kenna, sitting with her on a bench and holding her hand.

"Did you think it'd be this crazy, when we decided to do this?" I ask, and she smiles.

"This family is always crazy. It's one of the things I love

most about it," she assures me, and leans over to kiss my cheek.

Then she stands as Eli and Maggie get off the ride and I watch as her light-colored jeans get darker. Her eyes widen and I swallow hard.

"Your water just broke, didn't it?" I ask quietly, freaking out but not wanting to upset the kids.

"Yep," she says simply, staring at me with big blue eyes. "What do I do, Derek?"

"We grab the kids and go to the hospital. Don't worry, sweetheart," I tell her. The kids nearly throw a fit when I tell them we have to go.

"We'll come back soon," I assure them. "But right now, your baby brother or sister is coming."

It's total chaos at the hospital, with Eli and Maggie climbing all over the lobby chairs, but Kenna's parents show up after a few hours to watch them, and I all but sprint to the back so that I can be with Kenna.

She's already panting, trying not to push and I stand next to her and take her hand. She squeezes it so hard I think that maybe the bones in my hands will break.

"You're doing so good, sweetheart," I tell her gently, and she looks up at me with a frown.

"You did this to me," she says hoarsely, and I choke back a laugh.

"I did," I say sheepishly. "I'm sorry."

"You're not sorry," she hisses, and then the doctor comes in.

"I'm afraid the baby appears to be breach," he says, and Kenna goes pale.

"Does that mean a c-section?" she asks, and he slowly nods.

"Fuck," I curse. "Can I come with her?"

"Are you the daddy?" he asks.

"I certainly am," I answer proudly.

I hold her hand the whole time and Kenna looks up at me gratefully. "Can you look down and watch?" she whispers to me. "I want to make sure the baby's okay."

It's bloody and horrible and I think I might faint but I watch as my third child is born.

"It's a girl," the doctor says when the baby is taken out, and I'm just so grateful that Kenna is okay and the baby is crying heartily that I could cry.

In fact, I am crying, tears rolling down my face, and Kenna begins to sob after the relief having the baby out and everything going okay.

"Is she okay?" she asks. "What does she look like?"

"Beautiful," I choke out, finally letting go of Kenna's hand and going over to look at the baby.

We've picked out names already, Samuel for a boy and Delilah for a girl.

Kenna kind of has a thing for biblical names.

Delilah weighs seven pounds and six ounces, and she's utterly perfect, with what promises to be Kenna's blue eyes.

"They could change, you know," Kenna says tiredly as they put the baby on her chest after closing her up.

"They won't," I say firmly. "She's going to look just like my wife."

Kenna smiles up at me. "I am your wife, aren't I?"

"Now and always," I tell her, kissing her forehead.

Kenna's exhausted from the c-section and is now breastfeeding our girl, when she is done, I'll burp her and change her. Watching my wife breastfeed my child is a miracle in and of itself. It's beautiful. I missed out on that with Eli and Maggie, since Suzanna insisted on never breastfeeding.

Speaking of her, shortly after I proposed to Kenna, I

reached out. We came to an agreement. I gave her quite a bit of money, and she gave away the rights to the kids. We talked about it and she said she never wanted kids anyway, so this was really for the best. She had left us because she felt we were suffocating her and she needed to be free.

This way, she has her desired freedom and she can't come into their lives and wreak havoc any time she wants and she won't be able to sue for custody anytime she feels like she needs money anymore.

I'd been willing to pay whatever it took, and she took my first offer, so I'd say it's a win-win all around.

I talked to the kids and they said their mama was Kenna, so we talked and Kenna who cried a river when Maggie and Eli asked her to be their mama forever. We immediately started the adoption process.

Then, two months ago, news came out, very publicly, might I add, that Suzanna's new husband was filing for bankruptcy, and they were broke. Turns out he was involved in some sort of scam and was even at risk of going to jail. And so was she. She tried to talk me into giving her more money, but all her papers had been signed by then and money had already exchanged hands, so she had no rights and no way to demand more. I had no obligation toward her.

The final adoption papers were signed the day before our wedding. Kenna is now officially Maggie and Eli's real Mama.

The kids come to see the baby a few hours later, and Maggie cheers and Eli groans to find out that it's a baby girl, but they're both enamored with her the moment they see her.

She reaches out and grips both of their fingers with her

little hands, and they look at each other as if something magical has just happened.

I guess it has. We have a healthy, happy baby girl. We have our two other kids. Kenna has the big family she's always wanted, and I have my girl and my kids and I can't even find words to describe how wonderful the world feels.

"How long before we can go back to Disneyland?" Eli asks, and I chuckle.

"I'm not sure, buddy."

"Can we wait until Lilah is older?" he asks, already giving his sister a nickname, and I can't help but break out in a big smile, even though tears are still threatening at the backs of my eyes.

Tears of joy.

"Why is that?" I ask.

"I want her to ride the teacups with us," Eli says, looking down to marvel at his baby sister, and Maggie puts an arm around him.

I take a snapshot of my three kids and I plan to put it on the mantle and have it forever, show our grandkids. Today is more magical than any wedding, any honeymoon, even Disneyland.

Today is when our real family is complete.

Kenna's parents watch the kids that night because Delilah is a bit jaundiced and has to spend the night under UV rays. I sit next to Kenna's hospital bed and hold her hand, sleeping on the edge of her bed. It's uncomfortable and my back aches when I wake up, but it's perfect.

I've got everything, and I'm never going to let it go.

·   ·   ·

THANK you for reading Broken Single Daddy's Baby, if you like this book, you would love Grayson and Lilian's story Damaged Secret Daddy...

Read on for a preview...